Mary Elizabeth Moragné

THE BRITISH PARTIZAN

A REVOLUTIONARY WAR TALE

MARY ELIZABETH MORAGNÉ

Edited, with an Introduction, by

Bobby F. Edmonds

CEDAR HILL UNLTD.

The British Partizan
A Revolutionary War Tale

By Mary Elizabeth Moragné

Original Text 1838, *Augusta Mirror,* a periodical
Published 1839 by William Tappan Thompson
Published 1864, Burke, Boykin & Company

Copyright © 2006 by Bobby F. Edmonds

First Edition

ISBN 978-0-9749976-5-0

Printed in the United States of America
on acid free paper

This reprinting was produced from the electronic edition published by *Documenting the American South*, The University of North Carolina at Chapel Hill Library. The original book is held by the Rare Book, Manuscript, and Special Collection Library, Duke University Libraries, Electronic Edition used by permission.

Published by
Cedar Hill Unltd.
1000 Cedar Hill Road
McCormick, South Carolina
Email cedarhill@wctel.net

To the Memory of
Sally Edwards

Books published by Bobby F. Edmonds

The Making of McCormick County
McCormick County Land of Cotton
Destiny of the Scots-Irish: A Family Saga
The Huguenots of New Bordeaux
The British Partizan
The Neglected Thread

PREFACE

One of the jobs of publishing a book is to publicly acknowledge the people who made it possible.

First and foremost, recognition is due the author. Mary Elizabeth Moragné was a proud, versatile, strong-minded woman who outlived, not only her own generation, but the very social and economic structure of her time. She wrote *The British Partizan* at age twenty-two during the antebellum era. She sustained herself and her family with her remarkably durable intellectual and spiritual resources through the calamities of the Civil War, Reconstruction, and even into the twentieth century. Words continued to flow from her pen up to her last years.

I would especially like to thank Elizabeth Wright at the University of North Carolina at Chapel Hill for assistance given toward securing an agreement to use an electronic version of this novel. The University maintains an outstanding collection known as *Documenting the American South*. Thanks, also, to the *Rare Book, Manuscript, and Special Collection Library* at Duke University.

I am grateful to James Henry Bledsoe who has provided exceptional artwork for all of my manuscripts.

Thanks to the people who graciously assist in my efforts to market books as a self-publisher, including Vicki Dorn, Karen Bowick, Kathy DuLaney, Brandt Vickery, Martha Hughes, Dan Juengst, and Janice Grizzard.

My daughter Bonnie Franc never failed to provide encouragement and needed technical support.

My heartfelt thanks go to my wife Kathryn whose support is always lovingly present in all my endeavors.

Special thanks go to Phyllis Albert and Neil Bartley for technical assistance.

Finally, I wish to dedicate this edition of *The British Partizan* to the memory of Sally Edwards, who shared my love and adoration for the intriguing South Carolina hill country and manifested it in the historical fiction she wrote.

Bobby F. Edmonds
Cedar Hill, South Carolina

INTRODUCTION

MARY ELIZABETH MORAGNÉ won recognition for writing *The British Partizan*, a short novel of romance and high adventure set during the Revolutionary War in the vicinity of her native New Bordeaux, a French Huguenot colony in the hill country of western South Carolina. The story is based on the lives of real persons against a historically-accurate background.

The principal characters in the story are Ralph Cornet, Annette Bruyésant and Pierre Bruyésant.

Members of the author's mother's Caine family were the originals for the Cornets of the novel. The British Partizan himself, Ralph Cornet is based on William Caine, British sympathizer in real life. William's elder brother James Cornet, a Patriot (Whig) and the author's ancestor, had actually been killed by the Tories (Loyalists) in the manner described.

Ralph Cornet joins the British forces, but when he learns of the atrocities committed by the Tories in the region, he regrets his allegiance to the British. However, he does not join the American forces. Instead he exiles himself from his former home.

As for the British Partizan, "When it comes to riding, running, wrestling, or fighting, there is not the man in this country whom Ralph Cornet fears to face, hand to hand."

Lovely, proud Annette Bruyésant possesses "the soft exterior of the French girl." Young Huguenot heroine Annette Bruyésant and her father Pierre are both Patriots.

Annette Bruyésant's father, Pierre Bruyésant, colorful and typically Huguenot, is patterned after the author's own grandfather Pierre Moragné who actually came to New Bordeaux as a refugee in 1764. Although Pierre Moragné had little on his small farm that could temp the Tories, they took vengeance on him because of his outspoken remarks for the American Patriots. They raided his place often and in one raid he was shot in the leg by the Tories who were attempting to steal his horses. Moragné survived the experience, but remained in a weakened condition for the rest of his life. In the novel, Mary Moragné employs authentic dialect for the speech of the elderly Huguenot Bruyésant. The French father spoke "in a ludicrous mixture of French and broken English," which Ralph Cornet had no trouble understanding because he had known the French language from infancy, owing to the prevalence among the French settlers in the New Bordeaux colony, who clung with fondness to this last relic of their native country.

Patriot General Andrew Pickens, Lieutenant Pickens, Colonel John Dooly, British Major Patrick Ferguson, Hugh Bates and other Tories, appear under their own names.

The "vine covered" Bruyésant cottage depicted in the village of Vienna on the Savannah River the author likely derived from the home of Pierre La Brun, a Huguenot living in the river town at the time Mary Moragné wrote *The British Partizan*. La Brun's daughter Mary was married to Ralph Roland in the cottage by the author's beloved pastor Dr. Moses Waddel during a snowy blizzard on a December evening. Tragically, she died on the first anniversary of their wedding.

From the opening scene, the author skillfully establishes the magical Savannah River as an important symbol, tying it to the quotation from Sir Walter Scott, and uses it throughout the novel. The river functions throughout the story in a dreamlike atmosphere as the representative of nature, renewing itself and surviving even as the people suffer the calamities of brutal warfare.

BLOODSHED in the American Revolution began in Massachusetts and ended in South Carolina. That the last major action of the war occurred in the South was no accident. The British regarded the South as their final and best chance of crushing the rebellion. A southern strategy governed British military campaigning during the decisive years from 1778 to 1781.

In the southern backwoods and swamps was a savage, cruel civil conflict that pitted brother against brother and neighbor opposed to neighbor. Contrary to war in the North, where the campaign season traditionally came to a close as the days shortened and temperatures fell, in the South there was no winter's respite. War continued unabated.

After the comparatively easy captures of Savannah and Charleston, the British committed one serious, tactical error after another. They overestimated the number of Loyalists who would flock to their aid. They antagonized thoroughly the very people on whose eventual support they must depend if victory were to be achieved. Operating on the plan to subjugate southerners by using other southerners, the British precipitated in 1780 one of the most ferocious civil wars in history, where kinsman fought kinsman and neighbor betrayed neighbor. Loyalties in the war became totally confused. Civilians were slaughtered, homes and farms burned.

Historians assert that the British command never learned to fight effectively against partisan southerners in a land of intense summer heat and incapacitating diseases, vast woodlands, swamps, wide, deep, and unbridged rivers, and the impenetrable pine thickets. Here was a natural country for guerrilla warfare and an almost impossible terrain for classic European operational concepts. Ill-equipped, Patriot partisan guerilla fighters under brilliant leaders such as Elijah Clarke, Thomas Sumter, Huguenot Francis Marion, and Scots-Irish Andrew Pickens in South Carolina and Georgia kept the war alive in the South and ultimately compelled Lord Cornwallis to abandon his plan to invade North Carolina in 1780.

Southern campaigns were instrumental in securing American independence. By slowly bleeding the British, the partisans fighters helped forge the first links in the chain of events that would lead to Cowpens, Guilford Court House, and Charles Cornwallis' surrender at Yorktown.

AUTHOR MARY ELIZABETH MORAGNÉ, granddaughter of Huguenot refugee Pierre Moragné, lived from early in the nineteenth century (1816) into the twentieth century (1903). During her early to middle twenties (1838-42) she published both prose and poetry, primarily in the *Augusta Mirror*. William Tappan Thompson, editor of the periodical, obviously revered Moragné's writing. He praised her work highly and used her sketches, stories, and poems regularly, including two short novels, *The British Partizan,* and *The Recontre,* at least three selections from her journal, titled "Extracts From My Journal," "The Preacher," "The Dutch Wedding," and one long poem entitled "Joseph."

In the May 19, 1838 issue of the *Augusta Mirror*, its editor offered several prizes for original material, one for a historical tale "founded upon incidents connected with the early history of Georgia or South Carolina." Upon her brother William's urging, Mary Moragné entered the contest. She wrote *The British Partizan: A Tale of the Times of Old* within the brief period of two months. Her novel took first place in the contest, for which she won the complete works of Sir Walter Scott, plus a year's subscription to the *Mirror.* The story was published in four issues, December 15, 1838 through January 26, 1839.

Less than a month later, Thompson published the novel in book form. Apparently 5,000 copies were printed, priced at one dollar. Unfortunately, a flood in Augusta, Georgia, in May 1840 destroyed a large portion of the publication, according to Thompson.

The British Partizan received high acclaim from Northern literary journals and critics, the *Knickerbocker* declaring that it approached more nearly the style and genius of Sir Walter Scott than any novel that had yet been written this side of the Atlantic. Sarah Lawrence Griffin, editor of the *Family Companion,* in Macon, Georgia, wrote to Mary Moragné saying, "I do not flatter, when I say, that you can command a name which shall rank as high as any writer in the country, if you choose to do it."

In 1854, William Gilmore Simms, the leading literary figure of the antebellum South and a major American author, recommended Mary Moragné for inclusion in Duyckinck's anthology of American literature.

The novel was republished in 1864 by Burke, Boykin & Company of Macon, Georgia, from the original *Mirror* text, with a new preface by Thompson. The subtitle was changed to "Tale of the Olden Time," and Mary Moragné's name was replaced with "By a Lady of South Carolina." The war time, soft cover edition was bought by soldiers and civilians for seventy-five cents.

A decided change occurred in 1842 in Mary Moragné's blossoming literary career because of her church's disapproval of writing fiction and upon her marriage to Rev. William H. Davis, pastor of Willington Presbyterian Church. Her husband expressed his frank disapproval of her "tales," as he described the fiction she authored. Her interests were markedly altered. She experienced a great consciousness of sin, augmented by recurring periods of ill health. As a minister's wife, she broke off her literary connections and discontinued writing fiction, the art in which she was at her best and which would have brought her most fame and money. Nevertheless, she never gave up writing. She continued her journal all her life and contributed poems and numerous articles to newspapers, and to her church periodicals. She raised a large family and lived to age eighty-seven.

THE

BRITISH PARTIZAN:

A

TALE OF THE OLDEN TIME.

BY A LADY OF SOUTH CAROLINA.

———◆———

MACON, GA.:
BURKE, BOYKIN & COMPANY.
1864.

Cover of the 1864 edition of The British Partizan

TO THE READER

THE following beautiful Novelette appeared originally in the pages of the "Augusta Mirror," a literary periodical published in Augusta, Georgia, some twenty-five years ago, and for which it was written by its gifted author, a young lady of South Carolina, in competition for a prize offered by the publisher for the best romance founded on incidents in the revolutionary history of Georgia and South Carolina:

Through the medium of the "Mirror," it acquired a popularity at the time only limited by the circulation of that periodical, and what was remarkable in that day of our literary as well as commercial, if not political, vassalage to the North, it elicited the most flattering encomiums from the Northern literary journals--the "Knickerbocker" declaring that it approached more nearly to the style and genius of Sir WALTER SCOTT, than any novel that had yet been written this side of the Atlantic. To meet the demand for the story an edition was printed in book form, only a small portion of which, however, reached the public, the greater part of the edition having been destroyed while in sheets by the flood which inundated Augusta in 1840. Circumstances prevented the publication of a second edition of the book, and in a few years the "BRITISH PARTIZAN," at first so much sought for, had passed out of print, and in time out of the memory of the public. In reproducing it now from the pages of perhaps the only copy of the "Mirror" extant, the publishers are actuated not less by a high appreciation of its literary merits, than by the belief that it is a story peculiarly suited to the times in which we live. It is a tale of true love, wrought out amid the stirring scenes and harsh vicissitudes of partizan strife, in which the actors are the representatives of real characters, whose aspirations and passions, whose virtues and vices, trials and sufferings, triumphs and misfortunes, are developed and portrayed in an ideal history of intense dramatic interest.

But it is not our desire to forestall the judgment of the reader, nor to anticipate the pleasure which we feel is in store for him. One remark more, and we leave the reader to judge for himself how far we are correct in our partial estimation of the author. The "BRITISH

PARTIZAN" was her first literary effort. Quite young at the time, her first essay in the world of letters gave promise of a literary fame second to that of no female writer of America. But a second story--shorter but of equal merit--entitled "THE RECONTRE," also published in the "Mirror" was her last. In the very beginning of what must have been a most brilliant and successful career as a writer of fiction, circumstances induced in her a resolve, from a conscientious motive, forever to renounce a field of usefulness for which she was so pre-eminently endowed.

Reader, as she leads you, as with the wand of an enchantress, through this beautiful romance of "the olden time"--as by the way you dwell in ecstacy over her charming landscapes so vividly set before the imagination, or with the mind's eye look upon the varied characters with which she has peopled the world of her creation--so real, so life-like--and take to your heart the sound philosophy and elevated moral sentiment--not preached to you in chapters, but which like gems are strewn at random throughout these pages--you will, we feel confident, unite with us in the regret that one so gifted has not given to the literature of her country and the world, the fruit of her maturer years.

W. T. T.

SAVANNAH, June, 1864.

CHAPTER I

"Sweet Tiviot! on thy silver tide
The glaring bale-fires blaze no more;
No longer steel-clad warriors ride
Along thy wild and willow'd shore;

Where'er thou wind'st, by dale or hill,
Still all is peaceful, all is still:
As if thy waves, since time was born,
Had only heard the shepherd's reed,
Nor started at the bugle horn."

SCOTT.

"I fall into the trap laid for me;
Yet, who would have suspected an ambush
Where I was taken?

SHAKESPEARE.

WHO has seen and has not admired our beautiful Savannah? It is ever lovely, whether dashing in light ripples and foaming falls among the flowery precipices and purple rocks of Habersham, or whether spreading its broad bosom to the sea, still and wide, where the shadows of painted barges and smoking engines pass over it like the illusions of the enchanter's mirror. But in no place, perhaps, is its beauty more striking, than where its placid current stretches along the noble border of the District of Abbeville, its loveliness being there hallowed by the deepest and softest spirit of repose, which no sound is known to disturb, save the gush of song from a thousand birds, or the occasional recurrence of the wild and pensive notes of a boatman's bugle. For many miles below the "Point" where the "Broad River" of Georgia adds its tributary honors to the stream, nothing can exceed the beauty of the banks, whose massive foliage, relieved against a deep blue sky, bend over with graceful elegance, and dip their soft, shadowy archings in the untroubled waters. The Georgia bank is high, and mostly rugged; but on the other side is a vast extent of rich and fertile lowland, presenting at the time of which we are writing, a thick wooded level, where the Indian girl might well have loved to sit and weave her baskets of cane and bamboo, relieving her light task with songs, and twining chaplets of flowers. But even at that time, the song of the Indian girl had long ceased to vibrate in the echoes of that answering river. Her native valleys had resounded to the white man's axe, and her canes and flowers were crushed beneath the white man's foot. Poor child of the forest! In another land--if thy fabled Paradise is no dream--perhaps thou still wanderest by the semblance of that beloved and gentle river--happy that thou dost not see the reality; for to thee and to the nymphs of that stream there is no longer a home in its sun-burnt and rifled valleys. The genius of civilization has trodden upon thy sacred haunts, and with the materials of thy poetic inspiration built up altars to insatiate wealth--teaching this lesson: that whilst we are improving on the natural or physical creation, we lose in beautiful simplicity what we gain in art.

But, at the time of which we write, the "settlements" were principally remote from the river. A few families only had fixed their residences on its margin, and held by grant all those rich lands which have since proved of such invaluable consequence. The war of the revolution had been long raging, but the thunder of its cannon had only been heard in this remote situation, like the rumblings of a far off tempest; and though some of the most gallant spirits among the inhabitants of this district of country had gone to defend the Southern frontier, the many remained quietly at home, expecting that the storm would have spent its force ere it reached them. The event proved that these theorists were but little read in the politics of their own society; for the spirit of rude rebellion and love of plunder, owing to the divided interests and jealousies of a people so lately thrown together, without law, or attachment to bind them, had prepared Carolina for those scenes of fierce contention and domestic horror, which stand without a parallel in the page of history.

But man, in the pride of his heart, seldom values the "evidence of things unseen," and the miseries of the war which was deluging the Northern colonies with blood had not as yet visited the senses of the Southrons. It was owing to this circumstance, perhaps, that the hatred of the British was at this time less violent here than elsewhere. Their aggressions had been spared, and when at length they came with flatteries and promises, and unfurled the blood-stained banner of the mother country, they reaped their full reward of treachery and sedition. It was during the deceitful calm immediately preceding these convulsions, that a youth was, one bright morning, wending his way up the eastern bank of the river, in the vicinity of the scenery which we have just sketched. He was passing over ground which is now hallowed and memorable; for every particle of it is people with the invisible shadows of an acted romance. But the recollection of these scenes of horrid interest, is gradually fading away with the witnesses, and will soon exist only in the whispered traditions of their grand-children; yet there are some now living, who will recognize in the portrait which we are about to draw, the original of one, who, by deeds of wild and unequaled prowess, incorporated his name with the scenery of his native district, though it deserved no lasting record on the historic marble of his country.

The muse of history has woven her chaplets for the valiant and noble--she has even given to dishonorable fame the names of some of those, "Whose treason, like a deadly blight, Came o'er the counsels of the brave;" but how many, both noble and ignoble, have gone down "unhonored and unsung," their memory and deeds alike forgotten, except in its private records of affection or dislike!

There was at this time, however, nothing in the appearance of that youth, which could warrant the supposition of his future dark and wild career. His mien was gay and careless, and he whistled merrily, as he pushed with a light step, bold and free, through the patches of cultivated grounds and thickets of matted vines and canes, which in these degenerate days would be deemed impervious to anything but an Indian warrior or a rattlesnake. There was a determination in his step which bespoke a resolution that had never been "sicklied o'er by the pale cast of thought." It seemed rather the promptness of eager and untamed spirit, acting upon a mind naturally haughty, and impatient of restraint. There certainly was a princely superiority in his manner, as of one born to command, which would have seemed strange in a rude untutored child of the American forest, but that nature confines not her gifts to birth or station. The wild flower expands with greater luxuriance than that which is pent up in the gardens of princes--and the tall, almost gigantic person of this youth, in the power of its fullness and strength, and the beauty of its free, unrestrained gracefulness, might have shamed the kingly court of an Alexander amid the flower of its Athletæ. His garments, though rude, were worn with a native elegance worthy of his aristocratic bearing; and the manner in which a pair of silver buckles drew his small clothes tightly round the knees, displayed no common degree of vanity in those manly and graceful proportions. His neck bore further evidence of mighty strength--it might have become a gladiator--and it appeared broad and fair where the dark brown hair curled up over the edge of a fur cap thrown carelessly on one side of the head. The tout ensemble of the youth might have been considered foppish, if his features had not been so manly in expression, so classically beautiful: the broad open brow; the eye, full, clear and hazel; the finely curved lip, so proudly daring. But his eye, though hazel, had none of the soft characteristics of that color; it was fierce and sparkling, and seemed to aid the expression of scorn and daring, which mingled so strangely with the good humor that the power, and strength, and glory of early youth had settled into joyousness on his lips; for despite his mighty strength and stature, he was scarcely eighteen. His cheek, though slightly embrowned by exposure to an ardent climate, still retained much of its youthful softness. It was early summer, and the brightness and bloom on the face of nature, seemed indeed to testify, how much "this was fashioned for a perfect world" From the thick branches of the lovely syringa and clustering snow-drops, and from the leafy arbors, suspended like castles in mid-air, on the dark majestic trees, the sweet birds were sending up one unanimous exhalation of love. The white flowers were covered with bees and butterflies, and above their buzzing was heard the monotonous whirl of the tiny humming bird, as it pierced its slender bill into the rich horn-like flowers of the trumpet vine, which hung in festoons from the highest trees. Occasionally, through an opening, might be caught a glimpse of the river, just touched by the morning sunbeam; and in its still retreats, the silver trout would ever and anon break the surface of the water into rings of circling eddies. It was indeed a scene of harmony and peace, and it spoke to the heart of the youth with a familiar voice. As he advanced, with the dews and flowers falling around him, he appeared to feel an accustomed delight in the freshness of that early hour, which seemed to excite in him a sympathy for the vilest thing that could also enjoy it; for when the lazy moccasin crept slowly from beneath the fallen limbs in his path, or the wily rattlesnake glided off amidst the damp grass, he turned smilingly away and harmed them not. Sometimes he would surprise a humming bird in its flower-cup for the pleasure of restoring it to liberty, and once or twice he stopped to level the light rifle, which he carried in his hand, at a bird perched upon a high bough--the bird would wing its flight unharmed, but the bullet had grazed the spot where it rested. He was too happy to take life wantonly, but he prided himself as a marksman. And true it is that there was not another as sure of eye and steady of aim in all that country; for, like Hudibras, in logic, with his bullet he could "Divide A hair 'twixt south and south-west side." He walked on for some hours, and the sun was high above his head, when emerging from a thick copse of wood he came upon a smooth green plain, and before him lay the little village of Vienna--if five or six houses, rising in two rows from the river's bank, might be so called. On the border of this plain, where it slopes gently down to the river, stood a little vine-covered cottage, the refuge of a French emigrant, one of the many who fled from intolerance in their own country, hoping to find peace and the quiet worship of God in the shades of the great new world. Vain hope, alas! But as yet the emigrant had been undisturbed in his humble avocations, and was enabled to support, by the steady industry of his class, himself and an only child. This child planted his choice flowers, sang his favorite songs, and enlivened the little cottage with all the pretty playfulness and charming gaiety of the peasant girls of her own Amsonia. She could not have been happier had she been born a princess; for the wants of a false refinement had never invaded that humble dwelling with the longings, the discontents, and the jealousies of a vain ambition. The homage of one fond heart was enough for the simple wishes of Annette Bruyésant.

Thither our hero now directed his steps. He had, from earliest boyhood, marked this fair flower for his own, and with a gallantry which seemed to keep pace with his rapid growth, he had sought her love. No hand but his could gather her fruits and flowers from the wildest bough, and certainly no arm so well as his could swing the light canoe with such joyous rapidity along their native stream. But the gay devotions of the boy had changed into the comparatively silent entrancement of the lover, and many and many were the days that under the pretext of hunting, he had wandered on and on, until he found himself seated with his pretty Annette, by the cottage on the lawn.

"Oh, Ralph, I'm so glad you have come!" said the young girl, running forward to meet him, and then, as if ashamed of her eagerness, she stopped and hid her face in her hands.

"Are you so?" exclaimed he in the low, concentrated tones of impassioned love; and in the next moment he stood on the threshold, had caught the blushing girl in his arms, and pressed a saucy kiss upon her lips. They were so like twin cherries, an anchorite might have been tempted to the deed.

"Ralph Cornet!" said she angrily; for what young lady can bear to be kissed before witnesses?--it is so much like assuming power over her. "Ralph Cornet, who gave you authority to take such liberties with me? I shan't submit to it--I won't!"

"Who gave me authority?" repeated Ralph, mischievously; "why, yourself, dearest, when you promised on that beautiful evening to be Mrs. Ralph Cornet. Don't you remember, as we sat by the willows on the river? Oh, I have been so happy ever since! And say, father," continued he, as Annette turned off from him, "did you not give her to me?"

"Ma foi!" answered the old Frenchman, in a ludicrous mixture of French and broken English, "she would be sorri veri moch to dispute of dat, my son--ha! ha! ha! mais c'est egal; nevare mind, Ralph--de young demoiselles know alway, quand elles sont jolies. N'est-ce pas, Annie!"

Annette pouted her pretty lips, and placed herself with her back to the company, affecting to resume her work, but really with the intention of hiding the smile which she could not suppress. Ralph Cornet pursued her averted face with a smile which was wickedly fraught with the consciousness of power.

"Nay, now, Annie, don't be so prudish," said he, coaxingly. "I beg your pardon for it. But didn't you say you were glad to see me?"

"Well, Ralph," she replied, looking up gracefully in his face, "true enough; but you did not wait to hear all. The fact is, the village is full of strangers, and it was only last night that one of them came here dressed so fine and talked a great deal of nonsense to me, such as I don't choose to repeat, Ralph--Oh, it all amounts to nothing," said she, hastily, as she saw the rising choler of her lover, "but I thought I should feel better if you were here."

"He shall pay for it!" muttered Ralph between his clenched teeth.

"How, Ralph?" exclaimed the girl with an incredulous laugh, "you wouldn't challenge a British officer!"

"Ha!" almost shouted Ralph, starting from his chair, "British!--did you say British?"

"Oui," replied the old man, "c'est bien vrais--dey come here wid de compaigne of light horse--dey look so fine--mais! dey scare de poor peoples half out of all dere sens. Dey drink tout le vin--dey talk beaucoup--dey sing. O mon Dieu! Que des British sont mechants!"

Ralph Cornet sat for some time in deep thought. "Ah, if I had but fifty men!" said he, as if thinking aloud.

"Eh! quoi? Vat you shall say, Ralph?" asked the old man.

"Oh, nothing," replied he, "only I was thinking what fine sport it would be to drive these rascals from the country."

"Oui, oui," said the old man, impatiently, "if it could be done. But dey come here temps en temps--dey grow strong, veri strong."

Ralph Cornet rose and walked the floor, and at that moment a party of four or five men were seen approaching the house. They wore the British uniform, and their swords and epaulets, as they glistened in the sun, filled the fancy of the old man with images of horror.

"O mon Dieu! mon Dieu!" he exclaimed, with clasped hands, "nous sommes perdu--helas! I come here to find de peace, an' I shall find de trouble. Mais je sais mourir. Fuyer! my son, fuyer!"

"Be quiet, father," said Ralph, who, with his rifle in hand, stood in the door, a very imposing picture of resolute defiance.

The party halted within reach of Ralph's rifle.

"Hallo! there, young man!" exclaimed the leader; "in the King's name, what do you mean? You will not shoot at friends, I hope?"

Ralph dropped the end of his rifle to the ground, and the officer advancing entered the house. Seating himself without ceremony, he cast a hasty glance round the apartment, and a shade of disappointment seemed to pass over his pleasant features; but it was succeeded by an expression of curiosity and surprise as his eye fixed upon the fine, manly form of Ralph Cornet, who stood yet leaning on his small silver-mounted rifle, regarding the scene with an eager and dangerous excitement. There was something noble and pleasing in the aspect of the British officer, and to Ralph's unpractised eye there could be nothing more seducing than the grace with which the glittering sword and epaulets sat upon his elegant form. The penetrating officer observed this effect on the artless countenance of the young man, and turning to the old Frenchman, who sat in sullen submission, with his hands folded before him, he said:

"Well, old man, is this your son? Faith, he's a fine fellow; and I'll be sworn he has spirit enough, too."

"Aye, aye, and true enoff," cried the old man, drily. "Mais, he not be my son, for all dat."

"Ah!" replied the officer, pleasantly, "a lover, then, for your pretty daughter, I suppose. I'll wager my chapeau that she does not run from him! But," continued he, seeing the frown that was gathering on Ralph's countenance, "I beg your pardon, young man; we all have our weaknesses, and I confess that a pair of the finest black eyes that I have ever seen, drew me here this morning. Mais n'importe, as our old Frenchman here would say; we all have our crosses in love as in war; and, besides, this is no time to play with mammets, or to tilt with lips! However, I suppose you never read Shakspeare?"

"I am not much accustomed to reading," said Ralph, surprised out of his proud reserve, by the frank and courteous bearing of the young officer, "but when it comes to riding, running, wrestling, or fighting, there is not the man in this country whom Ralph Cornet fears to face, hand to hand."

"Ah!" I knew you were a brave fellow. What a shame it is that you should sit here idle, when there is so much fine work doing in the country. You should wear a sword and plume now, and command a fine body of troopers. How devilish handsome you would look in regimentals!"

Ralph's eye sparkled as it caught the gaze of the stranger--

"I should like it of all things," said he, "if I came by it honestly.

But"--

"You shall have it, by Jove!" interrupted the officer, eagerly; "you shall have it! With a few more such as you, we shall frighten the silly rebels to obedience, I hope, for I hate bloodshed."

"Grand Dieu!" exclaimed the old man, quoting a passage from scripture in his original tongue, "Ralph, tirez tes pieds des pieds des mechants!"

Ralph had been conversant with the language from infancy, owing to its prevalence among the French settlers in this district, who clung with fondness to this last relic of their native country. The officer, turning to the speaker, replied in an elevated voice:

"Old man, I am spreading no snares for my young friend here. A little reflection will show you that it is the best thing he can do for his country. What is the use of resistance? Our arms are victorious everywhere. Savannah is ours--Augusta is ours--and Charleston, your capital, will shortly be in our hands. The sooner we put down the few rebels left, the sooner will peace be restored to the country, and much misery spared."

The old man shook his head, and groaned audibly. But the officer had spoken with enthusiasm; perhaps he had deceived himself into the belief of his own sophisms, or thought that the dignity of his cause justified the means which he employed in its service; perhaps he knew that he was deceiving. But alas for poor Ralph! His youthful reason, which had never been taught to raise its eagle eyes to the sun of truth, was blinded by the splendid illusions conjured up by this master spirit, and his ardent imagination had already caught something of the ambition which burned in the eyes of the English officer. They were both so young, and congenially proud and fierce. But Ralph Cornet thought of his aged father whom it was his duty to protect--of his brother, absent in the American army, of Annette! That thought was last and dearest, and he turned coldly away from the fascinating gaze of the stranger.

The British officer was not a man to be easily turned from his purpose. Though young, his well educated and disciplined mind had an order and design to which he trusted for swaying the fierce natural temperament of this unsophisticated youth; for he knew that even the lion may be tamed by the power of the mind. He rose from his seat, and laying one hand familiarly on the shoulder of the young American, with the other he took the rifle and examined it with the eye of a connoisseur.

"By heavens, it is a fine weapon," said he; "I did not expect to see anything like it in this new world. It reminds me of such treasures as I have seen in the armory of England."

"It has slain many a deer in your parks," said Ralph, smiling. "My father is an Englishman, and did not come to this country without transporting some such treasures as you speak of."

There was a slight show of boasting in this speech, which gave the officer a new key to the heart of Ralph. He smiled, and said complacently:

"Well, we must be better friends. But tell me what is the most you can do with this beautiful little thunderer."

"Do?" said Ralph, archly, "I expect you would scarcely like to stand the trial of all I can do with it."

"Oh, I'm a fine shot myself," answered the other. "I should like to try a mark with you. Pray, how often can you strike the centre of a target, at a fair distance?"

"I can come twenty times within the eye, without missing,"

said Ralph.

"Gad! then you can bring down a bird on the wing?"

"Yes, or drive the feather from the top of a pole fifty feet high."

"Fore Heaven! you are the very man for me. Come, I shall stay here a few days, and we must make a trial of our skill. If you do not go with me now, I shall say that you cannot make good your boast." What entreaties or commands could not have done, this threat effected; for honor, with limited and ungoverned minds, is ever inconsistent. It halts at small matters and oversteps the greater. Thus Ralph Cornet to preserve his character as a marksman, betrayed himself into the hands of the British, even as the bird goes blindly into the snare that is set for it. Ralph knew not that he was going to his ruin, for with a cheerful smile he promised the old man that he would return that evening. In the easy familiarity of the stranger, he had forgotten that they were foes, and when he had joined his society, the gay life which the British affected to lead, added to the flattering promises of the officer, completely ensnared his youthful imagination, and he forgot his promise of returning to the cottage. If he had felt any regrets, the pleasant and accomplished Colonel Ferguson was just the man to dissipate them. He treated him as a friend; for there was in the frank bearing and undoubted bravery of Ralph, a dignity he was obliged to respect--but he left him no time for thought. For many days the British were seen riding through the neighborhood in light parties, and ever was Ralph Cornet mounted on a beautiful black horse, his own matchless Rover, by the side of the English Colonel, who entertained him with the "Pomp and circumstance of glorious war," without any of its concomitant evils. Perhaps being young and enthusiastic, he knew them not himself.

One day the British disappeared altogether, and Ralph Cornet was absent for the first time from his native woods.

CHAPTER II

"Oh, she had yet the task to learn
How often woman's heart must turn
To feed upon its own excess
Of deep, yet passionate tenderness;
How much of grief the heart must prove,
That yields a sanctuary to love."

L. E. L.

"Oh, Hamlet, what a falling off was there!"

SHAKESPEARE.

POOR Annette, the tender and feeling girl, wept the loss of her lover with the greatest bitterness, because, for the first time in his life, he had deceived her. Ah, those only who have permitted the stream of their affections to wear for itself a deep and powerful channel, can tell with what a sickening convulsion its whole weight is thrown back upon the heart, and how worn and dreary seems the course which it has hitherto pursued! In that first moment of exquisite anguish, a lifetime is compressed. The earth has nothing left to compensate for the trusting fondness of the heart's early innocence, or to return its withered pulses to their freshness again. The spring may bloom in vain, and the summer's sweets be felt not; for the soul can cast its own dark shadows over the fairest sky.

Thus thought and felt Annette, as she sat one evening on the green lawn before the cottage door. The light, yellow leaves of the beech trees were falling softly around her, as the breeze of Autumn whispered through them "In cadence low, a melancholy sound."

The river rolled within ten steps of her feet, washing the edge of the grassy slope on which she sat, and beautifully reflecting the rich masses of purple clouds which the evening sun had skirted with gold, as it shed through their irregular openings a soft luxurious light. But the scene had never been so painful to Annette; for all the fond recollections of her whole life, from its glad infancy, were connected with it. And now, as the stream of memory flowed back upon her soul, its waters were bitter as the fabled Achem. Her lips were compressed with an effort of grief, and her eyes fixed in abstraction on the western bank of the river, which presented one dazzling array of gem-like hues; for the slight frosts of Autumn had just tinted the maple and birch with the ruby and topaz, whilst the emerald oaks and evergreens--the latter now and then laden with scarlet berries--and the purple wild grape, dipped their nodding plumes into the clear lake-- like stillness of the water. But Annette's thoughts were far away, in search of him who had made the soul of this scene for her, and who, by his defection, had spread a pall over its beauties. So truthfully has a sweet poetess felt, when she said "It is our feelings give the tone to whatsoe'er we gaze upon."

Yet Annette wept not so much the absence of her lover as what she imagined to be his honor's apostasy. The soft exterior of the French girl covered a heart high and proud, which Ralph Cornet had in some measure formed in his own likeness--so naturally do proud hearts assimilate--but being more dispassionate, and with less ambition, she had clearer views of honor than he; and in the uncertainty and mystery in which he had left her, she trembled with horror at the thought--than which there can be none more deeply fraught with bitterness--of finding the object of her supreme affection unworthy of that love. The voice of fame was already busy with the name of Ralph Cornet. Several times had armed men been to the cottage in search of him, and curses, mingled with the word traitor, sometimes came to the ear of Annette. But she scorned the accusation with indignant unbelief; for the fond girl deemed not that the mind which she had ever looked up to as a master spirit, could be so warped from its native nobleness. Time wore on, and doubts, fearful doubts, forced themselves upon her mind. Why should he absent himself from her? and that, too, at a time of such danger; for the tories had began their nefarious works of pillage and oppression. Why deprive her so suddenly of his confidence?

As Annette sat gazing thus on the opposite bank of the river, entangling herself more and more in a maze of wildering and troubled thoughts, her attention was arrested by something moving among the bushes, and she thought she perceived the figure of a man swinging

17

from a bough over a little narrow inlet where the high bank opened like the jaws of a crocodile.

Presently the water seemed to be shaken in that still retreat, and a canoe emerged thence and shot rapidly across the stream, the feathery bark seeming scarcely to require an effort of the vigorous arm that impelled it. The figure which appeared was dressed in the British uniform, and a tall plume added to the giant reflection of his person, which the lengthened shades of evening threw on the broad mirror of the river. His coat, which was more than usually ornamented with gold lace and buttons, was turned off at the sleeves and collar with crimson velvet, and a sash of the same, very finely embroidered, girded a sword to a waist of strong but graceful delineations. Annette rose and leaned eagerly forward. The hat, with its nodding feather, was drawn far over his brow, so as nearly to conceal his face. But could she be mistaken in that form? It was he!

The heart of the poor girl throbbed with contending emotions: love, joy, fear, contended there with a violence that was too much for its strength, and sinking powerless into her seat, she covered her face with her hands, and wept as if that heart was breaking. In the meantime Ralph Cornet had sprung to the bank and knelt beside her.

"Annie, my love!--my own Annie! What, what is the matter?" he asked in tones of the deepest concern. But Annie wept more bitterly than before.

"Gracious Heavens!" exclaimed he, in alarm, "has anything really happened, Annette? Is your father ill?--or has any one --"

"No, no, no," interrupted the weeping girl. "But you, Ralph--how can you ask that question? Were you not my all?--and have you not ruined yourself and me?"

"My own darling, precious Annie!" said the youth, as he placed his arm around her waist, and drew her near him. "How can you say so? Do I not love you as much, yea, a thousand times more than I ever did! What can distress you so?"

Annette's cheek flushed high with unwonted energy, as she sprung from his embrace, and standing a few paces from him, she pointed to the plumed hat which lay on the grass with the last ray of the evening sun sparkling in its jeweled clasp--

"Ralph Cornet, what does that mean?" she asked in a firm tone.

"Mean, Annette?" replied Ralph, a little confusedly, "why, simply that--that I am a British officer!"

For the first time in his life his eyes sank beneath the bright glance of hers.

"Then what they say of you is true. You aided Ferguson in raising the tories in this neighborhood. You have accepted a commission under him, and you are"--she continued with rapid energy, whilst her whole frame quivered with emotion--"you are a traitor to your country!"

"There lives not the man who dare say that to me!" replied Ralph, proudly. "They who tell you these things, Annette, are no less traitors to their country than I; they have destroyed its peace and happiness by spreading rebellion over it; and if I have accepted a commission in the king's army, it is with the hope of restoring its tranquility."

"Oh, Ralph!" she exclaimed with clasped hands, "how could your noble mind be blinded with these falsehoods? You, who have been taught to love the very air of liberty; you, who have a brother now fighting for the cause of freedom!"

"Freedom!" said Ralph, "and are we not all fighting for the cause of freedom? But what think you, my little politician, is the freest state, the rule of one good master, or the lordship of a dozen petty tyrants?--for most like if we throw off the yoke of the king such will be the case."

Annette was not prepared to answer this equivocal argument. All her senses were bound up in the one anguishing thought of Ralph's degradation. She continued, without seeming to hear him-- "And then to be classed with the vile creatures who go about stealing and murdering. Oh, God! to be a tory!"

"By Heaven!" he exclaimed, with a furious gesture, "if I knew who had told you this!--Annette, I am not one of the vile things you mention. No, thank Heaven and my grandfather, I am rich enough of myself. I ask favors of no man. But if I was as poor and miserable as most of these abominable wretches, I should no less abhor their hellish spirit of gain. We fight for principle, but they have no motive save to enrich themselves by plundering. Do you not see the difference, Annette?"

"But you join them, Ralph; you excite them--"

"Our design," interrupted Ralph, quickly, "is to engage them in a fair field, so as to prevent their midnight pillage and murders."

A silence of some minutes ensued, only interrupted by the sobs of Annette. In that time Ralph Cornet's countenance had changed from its first expression of joy and triumph to one of sadness and perplexity--just as some fair landscape is shaded suddenly by a morning cloud. He knew not what to do with this strange and unyielding humor of Annette; but seating himself at her feet, he took her hand and endeavored to draw her thoughts from that painful subject back to the peaceful scenes of their happy and united childhood. It had a magical effect. Her hand remained passive within his own, and her eyes were raised with a sort of half smile to his face.

They dwelt there fondly for a moment. She had never seen him so handsome or so interesting as now, when he sat there in that brilliant uniform, unfolding a chain of bright remembrances, every link of which was riveted in her memory by thoughts of him. Encouraged by that smile, Ralph Cornet proceeded, but no sooner did he begin to talk of the future, than she withdrew her hand, and turning away her head, she said, in a voice so low as scarcely to be audible:

"Ralph Cornet, you must talk to me no more of love."

"Not talk to you of love, dearest?" said he, passionately, "when this tongue refuses its office, then shall I cease to talk to you of love. But surely, now, you jest, Annette; you did not mean to be so cruel?"

"I leave Heaven to decide which of us has been the most cruel," replied Annette, sadly. "I loved you, Ralph Cornet. I cannot hate you now, though I confess you have lowered yourself in my esteem. But you have placed a barrier between us. You will be despised and sought for by your countrymen. Even now, your stay here is dangerous, if they should discover you." Annette looked round fearfully. "And my father," she continued, with a quivering lip, "who loved you so well before--he has forbid me to mention your name in his presence."

"Ha!" is it come to that, already?" cried Ralph, starting to his feet with an angry gesture. But turning immediately to Annette, he said in a tone of persuasive tenderness, "But you, Annette, will not change, though all the world forsake me? I know you will not. You will fly with me out of the reach of that cruelty which distresses you so much?"

"Never, Ralph--never will I forsake my father while he lives. Besides, to follow you, would be worse than rash; for disguise it as you will, you have but an outlaw's life to offer me."

"No! no! Annette. I have plenty of resources; and if these should fail me, my right arm will not. I fear no danger. Go with me, my love, and then let them come, one and all."

"Talk no more of it, Ralph Cornet. It cannot be," interrupted Annette, in a voice so calm and passionless, that it chilled even the eager enthusiasm of the ardent lover; and he felt that no word of his, however warmly breathed, could prevail against the sober convictions of her judgment.

But, as if she had spoken the sentence which was to separate them forever, Annette commenced weeping afresh at the lonely and loveless future which presented itself to her view, and by an irresistible and impulsive weakness, her head drooped upon his bosom. What a situation for Ralph Cornet! The night was fast approaching, and he had promised to set his company, which lay on the other bank of the river, in motion by dark. But how could he tear himself from Annette? He knew that the faithful girl had not aggravated the dangers which surrounded him. He knew that every moment of his stay was perilous. He knew that he could not prevail on her to go with him; indeed, he scarcely wished that he might do so; for brave as he was, he trembled at the hazards to which she might be exposed in a rude and reckless camp. But it is true, though it is strange, that love can beguile the heart of man of its heaviest affliction! Even in that moment he was happy, most exquisitely happy. His arm was wound around her waist, and his lips were bent to hers in one long, long kiss of love.

But alas!

"How fleeting few are pleasure's moments! The brightest still the fleetest"--

That moment of entrancement was interrupted by the noise as of a struggle in the house behind them, and the next instant the report of a pistol was heard.

"My father! oh, my father!" screamed Annette.

Ralph Cornet stayed to hear no more. He sprang to the door, and bursting it open, stood with drawn sword fronting a scene which was but too common in those days. The dim twilight discovered old Bruyésant stretched on the floor and a ruffian standing with one foot on his breast, apparently deliberating whether or not he should dash out his brains with the butt end of a pistol which he held over him. The next moment the uplifted arm fell powerless by his side, and the wretch fled with a howl through the opposite door, where his two companions sat on their horses awaiting him.

This was one of the slightest effects which the false doctrines of Colonel Ferguson had produced in that neighborhood. The country was in a crude and uninformed state, ripe for sedition and outlawry. Perhaps no where could have been found a greater number of desperadoes than the extreme western part of this district, aided by the Georgia side of the river, afforded; men who eagerly accepted the favor of the British as an excuse for indulging their lawless propensities. The few Whigs that had been left in the neighborhood were unable either to awe or subdue them, because, like prowling wolves, they only left their hiding places in small parties and at the dead hour of night, incited by the love of plunder, revenge, or wanton cruelty. Though the cottage of old Bruyésant could offer but little to tempt their cupidity, he was no less persecuted by them as being an honest man, and an avowed Republican; for, notwithstanding his unprotected situation, the old man had expressed himself very boldly on the true side, a species of conduct which never failed to meet the prompt vengeance of the tories. Besides, Mr. Bruyésant had once very harshly refused his daughter to one of their number, and Ralph Cornet, though he knew it not, saved his Annette from a worse fate than she had ever yet anticipated.

That night Ralph reaped bitterly the first fruits of the cause he had espoused. When he raised the insensible form of the old man to place him on a bed, his hand was dabbled with blood, and on procuring a light, he found that the bullet which had entered the arm had fractured the bone. Annette, with her hands clasped, in speechless horror, knelt by the bed-side, watching for the first glimpse of returning life; but when it did return, it was with the frenzy of madness. All night long the sufferer was in a raging delirium, occasioned by the fever and anguish of his wound, and the spectre which seemed to haunt his distorted fancy was Ralph Cornet. Sometimes he called him by every endearing name, and would seem to be warning him from the brink of some dreadful precipice; then his voice would sink into low and muttered curses, and he reviled him with the epithets of villain, traitor, murderer, and called upon Annette to swear that she would never marry him. It was evident that Ralph was associated in his mind with the idea of his recent assailants, for whenever he approached the bed-side for the purpose of binding up the wound, the ravings of the afflicted man would cease, and he would shrink back, cowering and trembling with terror.

Groaning in spirit, Ralph Cornet sunk into a remote corner of the room, and awaited the light of day with the fever of impatience. Though he knew that daylight would bring no peace of mind to him, yet he felt oppressed by the darkness.

What a night was that for these two young lovers! They whose affections had been fanned into vital existence by the wings of that "unknown seraph," which, it is said, can make a paradise of any spot on earth, now found themselves together without the power of receiving any comfort from the beloved presence. Not one word of consolation or condolence passed between them. There was something so awful in that lonely night's watching by the side of a maniac!

Wearied, pale, and motionless, Annette lay at her father's feet, and closed her ears to shut out the sounds of that awful laughing and gibbering, whence reason's light had flown. The springs of hope and comfort had dried within her; and Ralph Cornet dared not approach her, for he had none to offer. With his face buried in his hands, he sat apart revolving his darkened and perplexing thoughts. He had already broken his word to his men and to his superior officer. They would move without him, yet he was equally incapable of leaving Annette in this forlorn situation, and of going to seek assistance for her from his countrymen, for he would be rushing to imprisonment or death. Near the hour of morning, the old man, from perfect exhaustion, fell asleep; and rendered nervous by the close air of the room and his unpleasant thoughts, Ralph rose and opened the door which looked out upon the river.

The first grey dawn of morning was rolling away the mists of darkness which lay like a folded curtain on the west, rendering just perceptible a thick vapor from the river, which seemed to rest like a dark column against the trees. As he stood watching its slow and regular ascent; with the cool breeze of morning blowing on his brow, Ralph Cornet concluded his first lesson in reflection. During the whole period of his happy life, he had never before had cause for one thought beyond the present, and his naturally strong mind had suffered from the enervation of a thorough indulgence. But that one night of experience had been to him more than years of common life--such rapid strides can the mind make under the stern proofs of adversity--and he stood there "a wiser, if not a better man." But, in the meantime, a plot was in process of formation against him. In the village of Vienna, Lieutenant Pickens had that night quartered a small party of militia, which he was raising for the State. At a very late hour a rap was given at the Lieutenant's door, and he was informed that a British officer was at that time in the cottage of old Bruyésant, and might become an easy prize.

When the door was opened the informant was gone, but with the first light of morning the Lieutenant proceeded cautiously to the cottage. A noise at the door disturbed the reflections of Ralph Cornet--

"Who's there?" he asked.

"Friends," was the reply.

Ralph hesitated. "They cannot know that I am here," he said to himself, "and if the tories have returned, I will not leave this spot."

But what was his surprise on opening the door, to find

himself confronting four men, whom in the imperfect light of morning, he discovered to be in the American uniform, and well armed. For a moment they stood there motionless--the seekers and the sought--and not a word was passed on either side. But in that moment Ralph Cornet had resolved upon what was to be done. Turning hastily to Annette, he whispered--"Farewell!" And seizing his hat and sword, which lay on a chair, bounded through the open door.

It was yet too early to distinguish features, but his superior stature and the boldness of his movements had awakened his enemies to the truth.

"It is Ralph Cornet!" passed from one to the other, and then there was a rush on both sides of the house.

"Shoot him!--shoot the d--d traitor!" were the words that reached the ears of Annette Bruyésant, as she lay in a half-stupefied bewilderment on the bed. In a moment she comprehended the whole of that fearful scene, and she sprang to the door with a wild, terrific cry. But they had passed on, and as shot after shot rang in her ears, the poor girl fell senseless to the ground.

Ralph Cornet reached his canoe in safety, and the thick fog favored his escape. His baffled pursuers heard the dash of his oars, but they had no boat in which to follow him, and they were obliged to limit their revenge to the discharge of their pieces in that direction. Ralph, however, contrived a feint to deceive them, and his shout of triumph reached them from afar, where he had landed down the river.

When Annette opened her eyes she was lying on a bed in the cottage, and a fair-haired, delicate young man was bending over her, with an expression of much concern on his intelligent features. A plain military coat was buttoned tightly around his slender and graceful figure, and a sword was buckled around his waist.

"Thank Heaven! You have recovered at last, Miss Bruyésant," said he, drawing a long breath, as of a person much relieved. "Your syncope was so long and deep that I feared for your life."

Annette looked up wildly. A feeling of painful confusion thrilled her heart on seeing herself thus watched by a stranger, and she covered her face, to which the blood had rushed violently, with both her hands. But as a recollection of the past events dawned upon her mind, she lost all thoughts of herself--

"Is he--is he?"-- she gasped.

"He is safe, Miss Bruyésant," said the stranger, soothingly. "He has escaped us this time. God only knows how much evil will ensue from it!"

"Thank God! O, thank my God!" she exclaimed, fervently, as she half arose, and raised her eyes and clasped hands to Heaven. The young man regarded her with a look of mingled pity and admiration, as she remained for some moments in this posture, with the silent tears trickling down her pale cheeks. The whole truth of her love for Cornet flashed upon his mind.

"Alas! young lady," said he, "how much worthy you are of a better fate! Has not this unfortunate youth done enough to forfeit your esteem?"

"He is so brave and noble," said Annette, warmly. "He saved my father's life last night, though he knew that he was his bitterest enemy."

"Ah!" exclaimed the young officer in surprise, and he looked round for the first time to where old Bruyésant lay, yet in a profound sleep. "Something must be done," said he, when Annette had related the scene of the past night. "You cannot remain here thus unprotected, Miss Bruyésant." Then, after a moment's pause, he continued: "I know a friend's house where you will be kindly received."

By his orders the soldiers prepared a litter, on which they laid the still insensible form of the old man. Wearied nature had sunk into a stupor, from which it seemed impossible to arouse him. Touched by the kind and delicate consideration of the young Lieutenant, Annette in weeping silence followed his directions for leaving that dear cottage for the first time in her life. It was now an unsafe residence, but it had been the scene of her childhood's innocence, and the sighs she gave were not only for her present distress, but for those "days of old," now hallowed by sorrow--

"For long remembered hours, when first love on her dawning senses burst."

26

CHAPTER III

"For there was breathing round him all the charm
Of high devotion to his country's weal;
And the bright panoply of gold and steel
That mailed his breast and glittered on his brow,
Gave proud assurance of a soldier's vow."
"He came to bid adieu--"

IN a grove of beautiful trees, about a mile from the river, stood a building, which, for the early days of which we have been writing, might have been considered splendid. It was large and lofty in its proportions, and though of rude and unfinished workmanship, from its superior size, the beauty of its grounds, and the richness of its furniture, it had that air of aristocratic pride which belongs essentially to the English gentry, whether on this or the other side of the Atlantic. But it was not more the seat of wealth and taste, than of kindness and hospitality, and in these troubled times the wretched found a shelter there from oppression. Yet it had not itself escaped the curse of that despicable species of civil warfare. All around was silent and lonely, where active industry and cheerful life reigned hitherto. The slaves were scattered like sheep without a fold, and the deserted farm-yard and broken fences of the trampled corn fields, bore evidence of predatory incursions.

A short time after the events recorded in the last chapter, two young girls were standing in the loftiest balcony of that building, which sat airily among the green branches of the majestic oaks, and looked out through their openings upon a landscape which extended to the river, and bounded itself by the hills of Georgia, in all their rugged and varied aspect. The river wound round to the north, and lay like a lake, with the waters sparkling in the sun; and a little farther on, where they through "arching willows stole away," a column of smoke, suspended over the rich trees, revealed the site of Vienna. It was a beautiful picture, in all its varieties of river, vale and hill, as viewed through the mellow light of a September morning. But the fair beings in that balcony seemed too much engrossed with more earthly feelings to enjoy the serenity, almost divine, of that aspect. It was evident that one of them had been weeping, and as the arms of the other encircled her, the afflicted one's head rested on her bosom.

"My dear Annette," said the fairer but not more beautiful of the two, "forget him; he is unworthy of you."

Annette Bruyésant, for it was she, raised her head from the bosom of her friend, and regarding her with a steady, sorrowful glance, she said in a tone which was embittered by a slight reproach:

"Selina Anderson, you have never loved!"

A crimson flush overspread the features of the fair girl thus addressed, even to her neck and temples. She turned hastily away, and her bosom heaved convulsively; but at length she threw her arms round Annette, and pressing her cheek to hers, she said in a soft, low voice--

"Forgive me, Annette, if I have seemed to distrust the strength of woman's love. Ah, I know its fidelity, through peril, disgrace, and aye, sometimes through coldness and neglect." Then sinking her voice still lower, as if afraid to hear her own confession, she continued: "I, too, love--one that is brave, honorable, and respected--but"--. She stopped and blushed still deeper; for it was the first time that the proud heart of Selina Anderson had confessed this much. Gifted with a mind above the ordinary portion of her sex, she possessed powers of endurance and concealment which gave a proud dignity to her manners; and those who saw her only in the friendly but reserved intercourse of social life, never dreamed that she sighed over a cherished but uninvited passion.

They had not left the balcony when a horseman rode into the yard. He was in military dress, and armed for traveling, as appeared by the pistols at his saddle-bow and the sword which hung in its polished sheath at his side. His slender, graceful form had an air of uncommon neatness and gentlemanly elegance, and his very handsome features expressed a singular union of feminine softness and masculine pride. But there were times when that doubtful expression fled before the noble daring of his high natural temperament. When he perceived the ladies, he reined up his fine steed, bowed low, and then springing from his seat, in a few moments was by their side.

"Fair ladies," said he, speaking in a tone of playful chivalry, which was rendered almost timid by his native bashfulness, "I have come to render you your knight's last homage before his departure," and he made a motion of lowly reverence.

Annette held the hand of her friend, and on looking into her face perceived that she had suddenly become very pale, and unable to speak. With the true instinct of a woman's heart, she instantly comprehended the feelings of Selina Anderson, and finding it necessary to say something, she enquired of the young man whither he was bound.

"I go, Miss Bruyésant," said he, "to join my brother at the block-house. We shall be called upon soon to co-operate with General Morgan, and I have come to beg the charms of your prayers against the dangers of war; for surely," he continued, with playful badinage, "the prayers of love can avail much."

Annette could not refuse a smile to this piece of ironical gallantry.

"You speak lightly of a very serious matter, Mr. Pickens," said she, "but if the prayers of a grateful heart can avail, you will go unharmed. I cannot forget that 'tis to you I owe my father's life, and the peace and security I now enjoy. May God bless you, sir!"

The smile vanished from the lips of Lieutenant Pickens, and he replied warmly:

"Speak not of it, Miss Bruyésant; it was but doing my duty to my country to succor the distressed; and may God forget me, when I forget her calls! But Miss Anderson," he continued, in a voice which softened involuntarily, "has she no word to encourage a warrior in the hour of battle?"

Selina Anderson had hitherto stood leaning against a column, with her fingers wound in a braid of her own fair hair; but on hearing this, with a faint smile, she broke a sprig of the oak which played around her head, and said with forced gaiety:

"Take this--and remember that Selina Anderson believes that you will deserve it!"

"Dear type of heroic deeds," said he with playful enthusiasm, as he received the branch, "may I never do aught to impeach the judgment of the fair one who bestows thee!"

A few moments afterward, and the young Lieutenant stood on that balcony with Selina Anderson alone. Annette had somehow or other disappeared. His manner now evinced an embarrassment but little short of awkwardness, and very different from its former gay and easy tone. There is nothing more trying to a shy man than a tete-a-tete with a lady under common circumstances, and Lieutenant Pickens had for a long time, most unaccountably to himself, experienced a secret uneasiness in the presence of Selina Anderson. Perhaps it was owing in part to the high and unmoved dignity of the young lady's manners. He did not analyze his feelings, but he felt that when called upon to address her by a single word he was more than usually reserved, and he avoided the slightest allusion to love. But the greater the effort to conceal itself, the more evidently is love betrayed. As has been most wisely observed by one who possessed a key to its thousand mysteries, "A murderous guilt shows not itself more soon, than love that would seem hid;" and it is doubtless a consciousness of this fact that makes even the bravest of men appear very cowards before the objects of their affection. The pride of the human heart is so easily alarmed--so sensitive!

Selina was the first to speak; for nothing oppresses woman more than silence in such a situation.

"You go so soon, Mr. Pickens?"

"To-morrow, Miss."

"And perhaps we may never see you again," said Selina, with mournful earnestness, as if she had involuntarily spoken her thoughts aloud.

The eyes of the young man fixed on her for a moment steadily, until they became tender in expression.

"And will Miss Anderson regret me?" he asked, in a low voice. The tone of that question restored Selina Anderson to herself again. The rich blood crimsoned her cheek as she thought of the warmth she had betrayed, and she answered with her usual proud indifference.

"Mr. Pickens would be regretted by all who know him, and certainly I, who claim the title of friend, might mourn his loss."

Her frigid coldness dissolved the enchantment to which he had for a moment yielded, and recalled the young officer back to the stern but high path which duty had marked out for his contemplation.

"It would be glorious to die thus, beloved and regretted," he said, musingly. "But, Miss Anderson," he continued with rising animation, "it is not the dream of a vain and selfish ambition which actuates our spirits. We are no tyrants treading on the empires we have crushed. Our country calls--it is the voice of reason, of humanity, and of freedom; and, in life or death, we are her's."

The young lady seemed to have caught something of his high enthusiasm, for her eyes sparkled through the tears which hung like dew drops on her silken lashes.

"Go on!" said she. "I feel that you will conquer at last; for certainly none but the God of battles has inspired that high and holy patriotism!"

"I doubt not of victory," he replied, with a smile, "though the prospect is at present discouraging. The friends of liberty will die in the cause; and such perseverance does not often fail of success. For myself, I go forward in the confidence of right, and if it demands the sacrifice of my blood, it shall not be withheld penuriously. Freedom must be established at whatever cost."

"Alas!" said Selina, "how much noble blood must be spilt to rear that sacred edifice! And those who have labored most may least enjoy its benefits."

"Yes, Miss Anderson. But the friends of liberty would answer you in the words with which our noble Washington replied to the suggestions of the Governor of Virginia," and the young officer's eyes brightened as he repeated that beautiful sentiment:

"What if I fall? my country's praise will grant my memory honor still, and if they fail to recollect, the God of Justice never will!"

Selina's heart beat thick and fast, and she held her breath painfully as she replied with outward calmness.

"Far be it from me to chill that glorious virtue. If I had a warrior's arm it should be among the first to strike for liberty. But life should not be thrown rashly even into a noble cause--and--and"--she hesitated a moment, and then continued rapidly, with downcast eyes; "and remember, Mr. Pickens, there are those who wish you to guard yours next to your sacred honor."

A bright glow overspread the marble brow of the young officer as he turned quickly and took her hand.

"Selina--Miss Anderson," he commenced:--the confusion on his cheek grew deeper--the half formed words of passionate declaration, which seemed to tremble on his tongue, died away unheard, and, pressing her hand to his lips, he rushed down the stairs and was out of sight in a moment,

"And is he gone?--on sudden solitude, how oft that fearful question will intrude."

Selina Anderson stood with her eyes strained in the direction of his flight, and when she had assured herself that he was indeed gone, her woman's nature conquered her forced and proud philosophy. She sat down and wept long, long. It was but a moment past, and he stood there with the confession most dear to her breast, trembling on his lips, and now, as he vanished from her sight, with the melancholy probability that she might never see him more, it seemed to the poor girl that she was tottering over a dark gulf, from which a ray of sunshine had suddenly withdrawn.

At the same time the high-hearted young soldier, as he was pursuing his lonely path, felt an emotion not much less lively than her's. He mused upon her words and attendrissement, so different from her usually dispassionate exterior, and a delicious sensation thrilled his heart with the idea that he was beloved. His own feelings, long repressed or unrecognized, arose with full force in his breast; but now, as he sped onward in the path of duty, he felt that he had "A rougher task in hand than to drive liking to the name of love;" and with warlike philosophy he endeavored to banish the tender thoughts which oppressed him.

But that which nature was insufficient to accomplish fate contributed to effect. The road he was pursuing was a lonely, retired path, leading over a ridge of hills for some miles, now descending into a valleywhere the world seemed bounded to a span, and again ascending to the summit of a hill as high as the tallest trees of the dell. As he was entering one of these profound hollows, Lieutenant Pickens stopped suddenly, struck with surprise at the sight of a beautiful horse which was picking the tender grass where a little stream struggled along, dashing against the roots of a tree or foaming among the masses of rock scattered through the ravine. The young officer was a great admirer of this noble race of animals, and a perfect connoisure in their excellencies, and he thought he had never seen a specimen more superb than that he now beheld. It was a horse of prodigious size and strength, but without the clumsiness that usually attends these attributes. On the contrary, the flexibility and grace of his limbs seemed to embody the "speed of thought." His flowing mane waved on the ground as he grazed, and his coat was black and shining, but as he lifted his head and recognized the approach of a stranger, by throwing back his small ears and snuffing the air with his wide nostrils, a white crescent appeared in his forehead, which relieved the uniformity of his color. Fascinated at the sight of so beautiful an animal, Lieutenant Pickens did not at first observe a man, who, enveloped in a horseman's cloak, with a cap drawn over his brow, stood in apparently deep thought, leaning against a tree not far off. When the horse by a natural instinct testified that they were not alone, the unknown raised his head with a start, and his hand instinctively grasped his sword. As he did so the glympse of a British uniform aroused the suspicions of the Lieutenant, and fully impressed with the belief that it was one of the many emissaries sent out by the British to incite the insurgent royalists, he determined not to let him pass unnoticed.

He first hailed the man, but receiving no answer he took a pistol from his saddle-bow, and advancing near him--for Lieutenant Pickens knew no fear--he demanded his name and motives, or the surrender of his arms. The next instant he felt himself in the fierce grasp of the stranger, and the contents of the pistol were lodged in the tree by which he had been standing. The slender form of the brave Pickens was as a reed in the hands of the other, but though thrown upon the ground with a drawn sword suspended over him, he asked no quarter. The cloak had fallen and revealed the British dress of the stalwart conqueror, and as he looked down with a haughty smile upon his prostrate foe, he said in a slow and measured tone:

"You have attempted my life, without knowing aught evil of me; but you are brave and a soldier, and I give you yours, now it is at my mercy. But, beware how you tempt again the desperate hand of Ralph Cornet!"

Pickens, who had begun to be touched by this noble conduct, sprang to his feet on hearing that name, and stamping on the ground in a fierce, ungovernable rage, he drew his sword, exclaiming:

"God! I will not owe my life to so vile a creature! Defend yourself!" Ralph Cornet parried his first lunge, and ere Pickens had time to make a more successful thrust, the knee of Cornet was again on his breast, and his face for the first time appeared convulsed with passion.

"Rash man!" said he, in a quivering voice. "Have I not said beware? Will you now promise peace, or shall I be obliged, for the first time, to dip my hands in the blood of a countryman?"

"No!" said Pickens, sullenly. "I acknowledge your superior strength; but we shall ever be foes."

"It is enough," replied Ralph, at the same time releasing his grasp. "I can expect nothing else. I do not ask for friendship; but remember, Mr. Pickens, that the man who has twice given his life to a bitter foe does not deserve the epithet of vile."

Lieutenant Pickens seemed to be struck with these sentiments in a man whom he had hitherto regarded as a ruffianly traitor; for he had never known him personally, and fame, in blazoning the bold deeds and evil principles of the young Cornet, had forgotten to speak of his youth, his inexperience, and his gentle blood. The American officer was no less surprised at these sentiments of honor than at the extremely youthful appearance of the man, compared with his gigantic strength. A feeling rose in his mind, mingling regret with indignation, to see this extraordinary work of nature perverted from its nobler purpose; and he said, with strong emphasis, in reply to Cornet's last remark:

"But you will acknowledge, sir, that you have deserved the hatred of your countrymen, not only for the evil you have done, but for the good you have left undone. You might have been --"

"It matters not what I might have been," interrupted Ralph, impatiently. "I will abide the consequences of what I am."

"Unhappy man!" answered Pickens. "If not naturally bad, you have been woefully misled. But even now, if you wish well to your country --"

"I might deserve the name of traitor, which you give me," said Ralph, with a smile full of scornful bitterness, supplanting the thought of Pickens.

The officer would have added something more; but the other turned from him, and calling his horse by name the animal walked up to him, when he threw on its accouterments, mounted and departed. Pickens waited until he was gone, with mingled feelings of anger, shame and interest. That bold man had so proudly subdued and scorned him, and with such lofty pride, too! But his bitterest thought was that he owed him the debt of a life doubly risked, and was bound by the laws of honor to take no measures against him.

CHAPTER IV

"A fellow by the hand of nature marked,
Quoted and signed to do a deed of shame."

THAT night, as Lieutenant Pickens sat in his apartment in Vienna, looking out upon the river and revolving in his mind the strange events of the day, an individual was ushered into his presence. He was a man in the bloom of life, yet in that period of its bloom when the fully expanded graces of summer are rich and pliant with the freshness and vigor of youth. He was short in stature, but slender and active, and his limbs seemed disposed, in a strong, wiry, fox-like suppleness. His face, which was ruddy and manly, might have been considered handsome but for a forehead "villainously low," and the sinister expression which very black, heavy brows gave to a pair of small, restless grey eyes. His florid complexion was very strikingly relieved by a thick mass of black curling hair and an Herculean beard. His nose was straight and well formed, and his full, rich lips, opened upon a set of teeth strong, white, and beautifully even. But there was nothing noble or elevated in his physiognomy; on the contrary, a smile of servility sat affectedly on his thick lips, showing that he was accustomed to work his way through the world by waiting the wind and tide of events; and his restless eye had furtive glances of cunning and treachery. He had not the air of a man who has much confidence in himself. His step was light and elastic, but it had more of the stealthiness of the cat than the self-importance even of the surly mastiff; and he had a habit of glancing suspiciously round him when he walked.

As he presented himself before Pickens he was dressed very plainly, with no mark of distinction, except that he wore the American badge, and his arm was bound in a sling. "Well, sir, what is your business?" asked Pickens in the haughty tone with which he usually addressed men whom he did not respect.

"I have something very important," replied the man, casting an inquisitive glance round the room.

"Never mind, Bates," said the Lieutenant, with a smile of irony. "Say on; there is no one here of more doubtful character than yourself."

"Your honor means to be merry at my expense," he answered with an unruffled countenance. "There is not a better whig in these parts than Hugh Bates."

"As occasion serves, I suppose. But when the tories are up to their elbows in plunder, and no fear of hanging, there is no better tory than Hugh Bates. Eh! have I not hit it?"

A dark scowl passed quickly over the countenance of Bates, which Pickens did not observe, and he continued: "But what is the matter with your arm, Bates? We have had no encounter lately, I think."

"Oh, its only a scratch that I got fighting with a tory," replied Bates, carelessly. "The devil was making off with the best horse in my stable. But I guess I peppered him--he! he! he!"

"Umph! umph!" said Pickens incredulously. "Well, it is all one, so you stick to the right side in future. But beware how you change coats again. You hear that, Bates. And now to your business. What is it?"

"I'm glad your honor has not forgotten it," said Bates, much relieved to escape from the other subject. "It is a matter of no importance to me, but of very great interest to the true cause. Colonel Ferguson has been seen in this neighborhood, and Ralph Cornet--"

"Ha! what of him?" interrupted Pickens impatiently.

"Your honor looks as pale as if you had seen his ghost," said Bates, with something of the "laughing devil of a sneer." "Do not fear, sir," continued he, still laughing maliciously, "that villain of a tory, bold as he is, will hardly attack us here. He is only helping Ferguson to collect the royalists in this neighborhood, and then they are to be off for North Carolina. But if your honor is not afraid to meet this lion, I can show you where you can grab these two friends and put all their plans to sleep."

The sinister countenance of Hugh Bates winced beneath the withering look of contempt and scorn which Pickens cast upon him as he uttered this last speech. Notwithstanding the characteristic softness of the young Lieutenant, he was subject to fits of arbitrary passion.

"Wretch!" said he, rising and stamping furiously on the floor, "dare to mention that word fear again to me, and you stand not there alive! I doubt much," he continued, as he paced the floor, "if you have not some other reason for wishing this man hanged besides your immaculate patriotism!" And his proud lip curled with the strong expression of his scorn, until it displayed the ivory teeth. "Ha! I remember now. Were you not the man who informed me that Cornet was at the house of old Bruyésant on the night that he was attacked by the tories?"

A slight change came over the face of Bates, and his eye sunk beneath the penetrating gaze of his officer as he replied humbly.

"I was, your honor; I thought it right to inform you of it."

"And how long have you known this man Cornet, eh?"

"Oh, bless your honor," said Bates, reassured--"we have been friends of old--he! he!"

"And you wish to obtain the benefit of that friendship by betraying him into our hands. Ah! I see it all," said Pickens as he walked to a window.

"Yes, d--n your eyes," muttered Bates between his clenched teeth as the Lieutenant's back was turned to him; and his eyes, as they fixed upon him, assumed the deadly glare of the tiger when about to spring upon its prey.

But in these few moments of meditation the young officer had formed a resolution which very materially changed the face of the matter. It was evident to his mind that Bates had some personal revenge to gratify in his persecution of Ralph Cornet; but he felt it his duty to have these men arrested, and as he was himself prohibited from leading the attack, he resolved to trust Bates with the affair; for the thought occurred to him that his enmity would be the surest warrant of success. Turning suddenly to where Bates was yet standing, he said with haughty calmness:

"Well, sir, how many men will you take for the enterprise?"

"Me? your honor," exclaimed Bates in real surprise, while a gleam of satisfaction lit up his eyes with savage ferocity. "If your honor would trust me in the business, I warrant that with four stout fellows I could take any two British officers in his Majesty's--I mean in this country."

"Well, you shall have your choice; but remember that your head will stand forfeit for the lives of my men, if you run them needlessly into danger. When and where do you propose taking these men?"

"Between this and daylight," said Bates. "The tories are to meet a little above here, at the upper ferry. Ferguson, in order to join them, will pass along the public road; for Cornet, not satisfied to go off without seeing that girl, Annette Bruyésant, has been down on a fool's errand to search for her in the French settlement, and they are separated from their party. I will station myself on the road and wait for them; and when we have these two leaders, what can the tories do, your honor?"

"By heavens!" said Pickens with a sneer, "your patriotism is truly self-sacrificing. Do you know the danger of meeting these men? Ralph Cornet is said to hold a heavy hand!"

"I have tried him before," said Bates, with a fiendish grin, and then continuing with an inward exultation as if forgetful that he spoke aloud, "and he shall feel the claws of the old fox yet!"

"What's that?" asked Pickens in an authoritative tone. "These men are to be taken alive; you understand, Bates--no harm done if possible. Alive, on your peril--you hear that?"

"Your honor shall be obeyed," said Bates, bowing himself off; but as his back was turned the whole of his broad teeth were exposed in a malicious sneer, and, clutching the paper by which he held his commission for that night firmly in his hand, he exclaimed: "D--n the preaching fool! Dead or alive, he is now mine!"

Penetrating as was the American officer, he had not calculated on the full malignity of the heart of Hugh Bates, and he imagined that by limiting his powers he should restrain him from committing any outrage against humanity in the business with which he had trusted him. It is a remarkable fact in the history of these lawless times, that however great the hatred to the British might have been, an act of inhumanity against them was ever revolting to the feelings of the American officers, and though Ralph Cornet had excited a bitterer feeling still, Lieutenant Pickens could not resolve to see him wantonly murdered.

But Hugh Bates had succeeded beyond his most sanguine hopes in his interview with his officer, and he went forth triumphantly and boldly to fasten his net around his intended victim. For many years he had been the deadliest foe of Ralph Cornet, and if he had concealed his hatred, it was for the full purpose of working out a surer method of revenge. From his earliest youth, Ralph had been a serpent in his path, which he wished, yet feared to crush. Until Ralph Cornet had grown into manhood, Hugh Bates had been the theme and boast of every gathering in the country. No man could contend successfully with him in running, wrestling, boxing, throwing the quoit, or in any of those games of strength and manhood in which the new world had established her gymnasium. But in every encounter with Ralph Cornet the latter had borne off the palm; and from the first time that he brought the back of the proud bully to the ground, the enraged Bates vowed in his secret heart that nothing less than the death of the young man could wipe away the stain of his disgrace. With every successive triumph his curses deepened to see with what lordly pride Ralph Cornet spurned the laurels which he had torn from him. His evil genius in love as in ambition, Ralph had also won the affections of the only being who had ever touched the vitiated but not insensible heart of Bates. But from the moment that old Bruyésant had indignantly refused to admit his addresses to his daughter, the fierce passion with which he had loved her was turned into a hatred, which called loudly for revenge on all who had come between him and his wishes.

He dissimulated his feelings until he could make a sure spring upon his prey, and his hatred germinating in the depth of his burning heart, produced a strong and living principle of revenge. He fed upon it--he slept upon it--he aggravated it day by day. At length the war opened an agreeable theatre for the views of Hugh Bates. The lawless rule of the loyalist party was congenial to his brutal licentiousness; besides, it was opposed to the family of Cornet, and without sufficient sentiment to become a partisan, he was a tory in the vilest sense of the word. We have seen him at the cottage of old Bruyésant, where Ralph Cornet, by a fortunate interference, again stepped in his path and thwarted him of his dearest revenge. Ralph Cornet's concurrence with the royalist party, instead of canceling the debt of hatred which he owed him only seemed to place him more securely in his power, and when on that night he fled from the cottage with a broken arm, he conceived the base plan of betraying him to the American militia, as already stated. The failure of that scheme was not sufficient to withdraw theferocious Bates. He dreaded to meet Cornet in a personal encounter, but he imagined that by joining the whig militia he could make them a party to his revenge, by working upon their natural indignation against the royalist leader. Accordingly he appeared before Pickens and enrolled his name with the company then enlisting. The actions and principles of Bates had been so secret that this new step excited but little notice among the whigs. Pickens, from his connection with the cottage scene, suspected more of his real character than any one else knew. Thus secured in this point, Bates kept a strict surveilance upon the actions of Ralph Cornet by mingling with the tories, who revealed to him unhesitatingly their plans and operations, and by this tortuous course he was enabled to spread his toils for his enemy.

CHAPTER V

"Then Hafed, if thou lov'st me, fly!
I pray thee, if thou lov'st me, fly!
East, west alas! I care not whither,
So thou art safe!"

SCOTT.

AFTER the departure of the young Lieutenant, Annette Bruyésant, on returning into the balcony, found her friend weeping. It had now become her part to console, or rather to weep in sympathy. The human heart, when left to indulge its sorrows in inactivity, sinks under them, and it is no doubt owing to the fact that in these perilous times the minds of the softer sex were kept in the constant exercise of active duties, that they showed uncommon strength for exertion and endurance.

A more than common share of the duties of life at this time devolved upon them. All honest men of strength and capacity had volunteered to meet the foe which was entering the country, and the aged and infirm left at home were afraid to venture out. The few slaves then in the settlement had become worse than useless property, and those that were not scattered through the woods were obliged to be kept concealed to prevent them from falling into the hands of the tories. In this emergency the fair daughters of the land--those tender scions hitherto guarded with surh gentle care, whom even the "winds of heaven had not been permitted to visit too roughly"--undertook, for the relief of their suffering families, the most menial offices, and performed them with unshrinking bravery and cheerfulness.

There are some situations in life, when the nerves being strained to their utmost tension, give a tone of hardihood to the weakest system; and there are many instances in the private histories of the families of those left open to the aggressions of the tories, of this latent fortitude, or as it might be better named necessitous courage.

Annette Bruyésant and her friend had not long indulged in the luxury of grief, when they remembered that the breadstuff had been exhausted since the last night, and there was nothing to provide for the wants of the family. What was to be done? Relief might be procured from a mill some miles off. But old Bruyésant was lying at the house, still disabled from the injuries he had received, and the only boy in the family, a lad of ten years, was sick of a fever. Then there was Clary, faithful old Clary, the only servant remaining to them; but she might be stolen or murdered by the tories. "We will go!" said the heroic girls. And now behold the two beings, who but a few moments before had nearly lost themselves in a maze of cloudy reveries, mounted on a little vehicle, half between chair and cart, to which was attached the only horse left them, and proceeding cheerfully if not merrily on their novel errand. The amusing varieties of the situation in which they found themselves divested the memory of their so recent griefs, so perfectly unnatural it is for the young and innocent mind to be sad while pursuing the path of duty. Enjoy while ye may, young creatures, for ye have yet much to endure!

They had seen nothing to alarm them on their route, and were returning with feelings of almost triumphant gayety to their home. They felt that they were bringing comfort to the sick and hungry, and joy to all by their gladdening presence. But scarcely were they arrived in sight of the house, when they stopped, and looking at each other with a kind of wild affright, the expression of their speechless countenances seemed to say, "the tories have been here!" No living creature was visible, but the broken windows, the mutilated furniture scattered in fragments over the yard, and the contents of the feather-beds filling the air, told the tale at a single glance. When they had partially recovered from their first exclamations of horror, the poor girls proceeded with slow and unwilling steps to the house, expecting momentarily to encounter the murdered bodies of their friends; but as they continued the search over these lone and desolated apartments, hope arose once more in their bosoms. Not a mark of blood was to be found, and the family had doubtless escaped. But they had left no trace of their refuge.

It was fast becoming night--a night of pitchy darkness--for the moon, which was by this time risen, found it impossible to struggle through the thick clouds which were distilling a slow but heavy mist upon the chilly breeze. In the pitiful and dread uncertainty of these circumstances, Annette and Selina wandered through the deserted place, searching vainly for a light or morsel of food. The work of destruction had been complete. Everything valuable had been carried off, and that which was not portable wantonly destroyed. Scarcely a piece was left of the elegant mirrors in which at morning these lovely girls had viewed themselves. The shelves were empty of plates. In one room a table was strewed with the fragments of a feast, mingling with broken glasses and dishes stamped under feet.

It was like haunting the chambers of the dead to them, and rather than remain amid that fearful desolation, they submitted themselves to the darkness of the night. Without light or guide or mark by which to steer their course, they took the direction of the river, supposing that their friends might have hid themselves in some one of the natural recesses of the deep wood. On they wandered, through the tangled mazes of the thickety vales and marshes. But no light broke on their straining eyesight. All around was darkness--silent, dreadful, profound darkness. Sometimes, indeed, as they scrambled through the deep hollows, an owl would send up his fiendish laugh over their heads, but no other sound came to "vex the drowsy ear of night." Fear, wild, agonizing, supernatural fear took possession of their hearts; their tongues seemed glued in their mouths, and every nerve strained and shrinking from the awful echo of their own footsteps. At length they sank on the ground, wearied and disheartened, and a stupor, occasioned by fatigue and the damp air, was fast steeping their senses in forgetfulness. But in that moment of death-like stillness, a sound of voices, very faint and distant, came to their ears. Nerved by hope, they sprang to their feet, and ran on in that direction. But the sounds seemed hollow and deadened as if they came from some subterranean abode, and often did the poor wanderers stop to assure themselves that they were in the right course. At length they seemed to be ascending a hill, and suddenly to their sight a broad glare came up from the earth, spreading a ghastly yellow glow over the leaden sky and the sombre foliage of the giant trees; but what was their horror on discovering beneath them the very objects from which they were flying!

The hill or bank on which they stood extended round for many feet perpendicularly below them, forming a kind of circular barrier for the river which in high water overflowed the enclosure. Tall trees grew up from the loamy soil, but the undergrowth was wanting, and the space beneath was strewed with fallen trees, dried sticks and leaves. Its naturally gloomy aspect was now rendered fearfully wild by the effect of the various lights scattered through it, around which sat or stood about thirty or forty ferocious looking beings, in every variety of grotesque attitudes. Several groups of four and five were seated at cards round an old log or stump, in which they had placed a rosin torch, very ingeniously sheltered from the night air by a piece of bark--and every few minutes they stopped to curse their luck, or the rain, which fell occasionally in soft showers, wetting them through by slow degrees. Some had burnt coal fires under the logs, by which they sat cooking and eating; and others had kindled blazing fires by piling up heaps of the dried sticks and faggots, around which they circled in irregular measures, singing, shouting, and brandishing their empty bottles over dark countenances, which were rendered fiendish by contrast with the red handkerchiefs tied carelessly around them.

Fascinated by a spectacle so novel, the poor fugitives crouched closely behind a large tree in breathless curiosity. Just beneath them, on the ground, sat two men, who seemed, by some marks of distinction, to be the leaders of the band. Their swords lay beside them, and hats with red feathers sat jauntily on their rugged, sun-burnt features, which were strongly illumined by the light.

"Ha! ha! ha!" laughed one of them in a coarse, rough voice, so near that the frightened girls heard distinctly every tone, "How these rascals do gig it," said he, "they would sell themselves to the devil for a bottle of whisky."

"Damn it, Johnson!" said the other, "you needn't say a word; we've all had our share of the fat things at the big house yonder, to-day. How the poor devils did run! But as for belonging to the old fellow below there, that you speak of, I think I know somebody who will be apt to go there himself, to pay for a barrel of jewels and trumpery which the old woman had buried on the river bank."

"Ha! ha!" again laughed the brutal Johnson. "That was the best thing I ever done, Georgie, except it was skinning that old black rascal alive, when he wouldn't tell me where his master was."

"Yes," replied the other, who was known by the familiar title of Georgie Long, "and if you are not damned for that, you will be for blowing out the brains of the little brat who caught hold of the blanket you was pulling off of him."

"Well, Georgie," said he, rising from his elbow with an unmoved and hardened smile, "we have both done enough to damn us; but no matter--its high time we were moving. You know we promised to meet Ferguson at the ferry, and if we wait till day-light we might chance to fall in with some of the d--d rebels. I'll be sworn they have the scent of us by this time."

"And Cornet, Captain Cornet, is to lead us into North Carolina," said Long. "He seems to be in high favor. But do you feel like knocking under to this proud, beardless--"

A deep groan from the top of the hill arrested this speech. "Who's there?" shouted the two men, as they sprang simultaneously to their feet.

In a few moments one half the tories had scoured the hill. But the unfortunate objects of their alarm had fled, with footsteps winged by fear, far from the tory camp. Their feet were bruised, their garments torn, but they knew not where to stop; and in the delirium of their fears and confusion they ran on and on, far as possible from the direction they had at first taken, until one of them stumbled over something and fell with a scream to the ground.

"Mercy! mercy! ye wad na take an auld man's life?" said a voice in a broad Scotch accent, as something seemed struggling from the ground.

"Heavens be thanked!" said Annette Bruyésant, with a long, deep inspiration of her suspended breath. "It is the voice of old Andrew Morrison, the miller!"

"Yes, it is auld Andrew Morrison," said the man, whose senses were not yet clear of the vapors of sleep, "and what harm has puir auld Andrew ever din ye, I maun ask?"

"For shame, Andrew, rise. It's I, Annette Bruyésant."

"Oh, an' is it yersel', Miss Annie? Then it canna be the tories! Guid be praised for a' his mercies! Bless yer bonnie face," he continued, "how caum ye here, yer lone sel', this waefu' night. Hae ye nae beem hame, syne?"

"Yes, Andrew, but the tories have sent our friends to the woods, and we did not know where to find them?"

"Bless the puir childer! And ye hae na hame, then?" said the kind hearted Andrew. "I guessed some e'il wad come to ye. Sae when ye had left the mill aboon, I said to mysel', I maun see the bonny leddies safe hame; but jist as I was ganging on the road hard bye, I heard the tramp o' feet, and as I dinna ken whether frien or fae, I turned in here a bit to rest mysel' 'til day--. But the Lord defend us, Miss Annie, wha's here?" continued old Andrew, as he stooped and raised from the ground the form of Selina Anderson, who, through fatigue and fear, had fainted.

Annette supported her in her arms, and seeing she did not speak, the old man groped about for a stream, which he knew was close by, and bringing the water in his hat, threw some in her face. When she had a little revived, he spread his coat on the grass, and begging them to lie down and rest he started off, saying kindly--

"Ye maun bide here young leddies till I come back. I will bring ye to yer freins."

Worn out with fatigue, the poor wanderers folded in each other's arms, sank into a deep sleep. When they awoke morning had opened on the horizon, and was chasing, with successive shades of rose and orange, the dark clouds of the night away to the west. Then all rolled off, and no stain was left on the delicate azure, whence the bright, beautiful star of morning looked down upon them, like the smiling and benignant eye of the All-seeing One.

Chilled with the damp air of the night, they arose and walked out into the road. The old man had not yet returned. Of course he had not found their friends, and, accustomed to act for themselves, and wearied of suspense, they determined to follow the road until they reached Vienna, where they might expect to find assistance.

They had not proceeded far when they were overtaken by two

horsemen. One hasty glance behind assured them that they were in the uniform of British officers, and the poor girls turned modestly aside to suffer them to pass. But that one glance had been sufficient--in the next moment Ralph Cornet was kneeling before Annette. He had forgotten the bitterness of their last meeting, his own circumstances, and the presence of witnesses, in the surprise, the rapture, the agony of seeing her again.

He caught her hand between both his own. "Oh, Annette!" he said, "where have you been? I have sought you everywhere."

With a faint scream, Annette's head sunk on the bosom of her friend, and she made an effort to withdraw her hand. Ralph relinquished it, and turned away his head, much aggrieved--

"You will not speak to me, Annie?" he said in a tone of reproof so touching that she burst into tears.

"Young gentleman," said Selina Anderson, who was vexed at Annette's distress, "if I judge rightly you are Mr. Cornet; if so, you had best leave us. This is a dangerous place for you. As for Miss Bruyésant, whatever kind remembrances she may have for you, she can never look with favor on the man who herds with the destroyers of her country, and who gives his countenance and support to the merciless robbers that send her friends into the woods penniless wanderers."

"Heavens!" said Ralph eagerly, "you are not thus?"

"Yes," replied the young lady, with bitter emphasis, "thanks to the courtesies of your friends, we have been all night seeking ours from whom we have been separated."

Ralph Cornet stood for a moment with his brow knit and his lips compressed, until he scarcely seemed to breathe. Perhaps till that moment he had never known the bitterness of his situation; for he felt that he could not revenge that outrage. But he turned round calmly--

"I am not the ruffian you take me for," said he, in a subdued voice.

"If they have driven you from your homes, it is my duty to restore you to them. Your friends have taken to the woods, did you say?" Selina answered proudly, as if she would have disdained the proffered service, but Ralph affected not to notice it.

"Colonel Ferguson," said he to the officer who sat on horseback, viewing the scene with eager interest, "you can either await me here, or go on."

"Heaven forbid, Cornet, that I should prove so recreant a knight as to retire from such a gallant enterprise," exclaimed the accomplished Englishman, leaping from his saddle. "If," continued he, bowing gracefully, "if these young ladies will accept my services--"

"No! no!" Ralph Cornet, you shall not go!" exclaimed Annette, starting up wildly. "They hate you!--they seek for you! You go to certain death!"

"I fear no danger for my young friend but that of your presence, Miss Bruyésant," said Colonel Ferguson. "For all others I would trust his ingenuity and daring."

"Trust me, Annette," said Ralph, with a bitter smile. "I will see you in safety before I die. I know these woods--follow me."

Ralph Cornet led the way, and Colonel Ferguson, with the rein of his bridle thrown over his arm, walked by the side of Selina Anderson, whom, in spite of her prejudices, he had already began to interest by the graces of an elegant mind and noble soul.

"You are the sister of an American General," said he at length, "and you are worthy of being so. You will be surprised, young lady, to hear that I respect your feelings and your pride; but hereafter, whenever you hear the name of Ferguson mentioned, do him the justice to say that he admired the enemy it was his misfortune to oppose."

They had, however, proceeded but a short distance in this way, when they were met by old Andrew Morrison. He had found the camp and was returning. The old Scotchman stopped short on seeing them; but Ralph advanced and shook him cordially by the hand.

"Ah, Ralph, Ralph!" said he, in reply to that familiar salutation, "Sic waefu times! sic waefu times! Wha wad hae thought to hae seen yer manfu' limbs in British gear--ye that waur aye sae kind to a' --"

"Hush, hush! Andrew, for Heaven's sake," said Ralph, impatiently.

"Na, na! I wadna hush, Ralph, when yer ain life is at stake. Turn back this instant and flee; for the tories hae been up at their e'il doings and the militia men are out. They will be here fu' sune, for they hae heard that ye wad pass this way. Flee, Ralph, flee! A'e moment mair and I dinna ken what may betide."

"I've sworn to see them safe," said Ralph sullenly, "and I will die in the attempt."

"Wha? these bonny leddies? Bless yer kind heart, they are safe enough wi' auld Andrew. The camp is hard by. Dinna gang there, boy. On the word of an auld man, wha has lo'ed ye frae the time ye hae sat on his knee, a canny child--awa! awa! Ye waur aye kind to an auld body, an' --"

At that instant the tramp of horses' feet was heard on the dry sticks and leaves of the forest.

"Whist! whist! my boy! Wat ye wha's coming?" continued old Andrew, fearfully.

Ralph seemed to rouse himself painfully from a fit of musing. He turned and wrung the hand of the old man.

"They are safe, you say, Andrew Morrison?"

"Awa'! awa'! Ralph, for your life!" repeated Andrew, in a tone of the most impatient alarm, for the tramping came nearer and nearer. Ralph's presence of mind never forsook him in the hour of danger, and though in the obstinate daring of his nature he would have faced a host, and died to serve the object of his love, he was clear-sighted enough to perceive the utter folly, the madness of drawing himself and his friend into further peril. Without more deliberation he sprung into his saddle, and motioning the astonished Ferguson to do the same, he made for the road they had left, without trusting himself with even a look at the wondering girls. But it was too late--the Americans were near enough to catch a glimpse of British uniforms, and already a sharp report rang through the woods.

"Great God!" exclaimed Ferguson, as his horse fell under him in the convulsive motion of death, "I am lost!" Ralph Cornet looked behind him and sprang to the ground.

"Here, Ferguson! Take this horse, and fly for your life!" said he.

"God of Heaven!" exclaimed Ferguson, passionately, "and leave you to perish?"--

"Not one word more," said Ralph, with solemn earnestness. "Fly! or we are both lost; for I swear not to quit this spot till you are gone! Fear not for me--but take care of Rover till I see you."

Ferguson looked vexed and puzzled at the stubborn resolution of Ralph. But by this time the foremost man, who discharged his gun, was grappling with Ralph, and as Ferguson saw him dash his opponent to the ground and fly through the woods, he mounted that good steed, for the others were close at his heels. Two men followed him, but there were few horses in those days that could compete with Ralph Cornet's well-trained Rover, and they soon returned to join the chase of the other fugitive. Hugh Bates, for it was he whom Cornet had again foiled, sprang lightly to his feet, and his face was livid with rage. He grasped only the sword of Ralph Cornet, which he had borne away in the struggle.

Mounting his horse, he struck his rowels into its flanks, and, with a shout to his comrades, he flew after his adversary. Once they came in sight of him, and to make "assurance doubly sure," every gun was leveled and discharged; but with a bound like the deer that bears his death wound, Ralph fled with greater speed than before. Able at any time, on fair ground, to distance the fleetest runner, the thick woods and broken country were now an advantage to the wounded man. They lost sight of him altogether, but like blood-hounds they followed on that bloody track.

Once again they saw him on the border of a cornfield, and as he turned to look he staggered. The pursuers rushed on with a shout of exultation. But when they had struggled through the cane-brake to the banks of the river, he was nowhere visible. There were fresh tracks on the soft soil, and a bloody glove lay close by the edge of the stream. A canoe was also lying there, half buried in the leaves which carpeted the surface of the quiet river, upon which the early sunbeams were glancing, betraying not by a single ripple that any object had lately disturbed its tranquility. What a contrast was that placid river to the boiling blood of those hot pursuers! But theirs were not the "high hearts" to see and feel its "eloquence and beauty."

All night long they had ridden on the pursuit, and now, in the fury of their baffled revenge, they scoured the banks of the river. But there was no trace of Ralph Cornet on land, and supposing that he might have resorted to the stratagem of diving, they stationed themselves on each side of the stream, prepared to shoot him down as he emerged from the water.

All day, so bitter was their hatred, did they watch. But night came, and they departed sullenly, to spread the report of his death. Arguing from the impossibility of his having crossed the river ere they reached it, they believed that he must have drowned himself in a fit of desperation or exhaustion; and for many days, Hugh Bates, whose enmity reached beyond the limits of death itself, searched along that river for the body.

Ferguson, who had arrived safely, and met his company at the appointed rendezvous, lingered a day or so; but his emissaries all returned with the story of Ralph's mysterious disappearance, and the British Colonel led on where his duty called him. But he reproached himself with the misfortunes of that brave, misguided youth. He did more--he shed for him the manly tears of sympathy, for he had discovered the worth of the noble heart which he had been instrumental in corrupting.

In his own neighborhood, Ralph Cornet's death was currently reported, attended with supernatural awe among the ignorant and superstitious. Some said that an evil spirit had carried him off, and his name was used to frighten children. But there was one who heard these things with indignation. She believed not the tale of her lover's death; so great was her confidence in his powers, and so easily can the young heart be illumined by the slightest ray of hope. Conviction only, feeling, sensible conviction, alone can extinguish it.

For a length of time Annette wandered out every day alone. She shunned even the company of Selina Anderson. Something whispered to her heart that Ralph was yet alive, that he would seek an interview with her. But one day she came upon the place where he had fled before his pursuers to the river. The traces of blood remained there still, and even the glove had not been removed.

These mournful tokens seemed to bring to the mind of the

affectionate girl the conviction she had so long shunned, and she sat down and wept over them in bitterness of soul. She forgot his errors and his degradation. She thought of him only as the brave and beautiful boy--the sweet companion of her childhood--as the manly youth--the elected husband of her young affections. Who could blame that young girl if in such a moment she forgot that he had been unfaithful to his country?

CHAPTER VI

"Let laurels, drenched in Pernassian dews,
Reward his mem'ry dear to every muse,
Who with a courage of unshaken root,
In honor's field advancing his firm foot,
Plants it upon the line that justice draws,
And will proceed or perish in her cause."
"They sin who tell us love can die!"

MONTHS rolled on, and nothing was heard of Ralph Cornet. He had ceased to be classed among the living; but his memory had not passed away with all. In one heart the altar of his worship was still fed with the daily sacrifice of prayers and tears; and as its fire burnt on in secret the fair priestess seemed to become less and less earthly. Her mind, like that dove which hovered over the wide waste of waters, found no green leaf for a resting place on earth, and it dwelt among the invisible shadows of the past.

Yet Annette Bruyésant refused to believe in the death of her lover. She had not seen him die; and in the slow, torturing fire of unlimited suspense, her once rosy cheek paled, and her rounded form became every day more and more attenuated and sylph-like.

The spring was far advanced--that dreadful spring of 1781. The tories who had escaped from the fatal rencontre of King's Mountain, had returned into the neighborhood, and literally ravaged it with fire and sword. The whigs were led on by desperation to return the aggression, and murders were committed and revenged, until many of the families of the whigs, who were far in the minority, were left without protectors and without food--the crops of the last year having been destroyed--and despair seemed to have benumbed the energies of the wretched survivors.

At this crisis an individual came to the relief of the suffering inhabitants, and with a generous assiduity, a self-sacrificing zeal, to which history has not and never can do justice, he succored the destitute women and children. Many a "verdant offering to his memory" has been perpetuated in the children of those who felt his protecting benevolence. This man was Gen. Pickens.

On the bank of the river, a little apart from Vienna, may yet be seen the remains of a fort which was built for the defense of the early settlers against the Indians. Its walls were built of stone, and formed ten feet high, with port-holes and other appliances of stout resistance. Here Gen. Pickens supported his dependents, and old age and infancy flocked daily to his protecting care. But thanks to the cowardice of the tories, and their successive defeats in open combat, this weak garrison was in no danger of attack. It was more like the residence of a pleasant family than a warlike station; and during his occasional visits the "good General," as he was affectionately called, added to the charm of an universal cheerfulness; for he was not more eminent for the soldier-like qualities which gained him the distinction of an officer, than for the gracious affability by which he won all hearts. The victory of the Cowpens had given a breathing space to the militia of the General's brigade. Most of them had returned on parole to their families, and the General took occasion at this time to visit Fort Charlotte, which was the name given to the fortress by the loyal subjects of his Majesty, George the Third.

The concentration of the British on the other side of the District lulled the inhabitants into an easy security, and the fort was consequently under but few of the restraints which martial discipline imposes. General Pickens was walking one night alone and meditatively, on the outer side of the wall, when he perceived the figure of a man leaning against it, in the deep shadow which the dark trees opposed to the moonlight. Having hailed him several times and received no answer, the General took a pistol from his pocket and walked up to the spot to assure himself that he had not been deceived.

"Speak, or you are my prisoner," said he, as he approached the stranger.

The man made no show of resistance, but as the General was about to lay his hand on his shoulder he retreated a few paces, and folding his arms on his breast, answered doggedly:

"Shoot, if you will. I will be no man's prisoner."

As he stepped back, the moonlight streamed clear upon a majestic form, and showed the bold outline of a countenance which looked pale and melancholy, in that pensive light.

General Pickens looked at him a few moments in silence. The subdued and sad expression of his features and attitude seemed to have awakened in his heart some feeling of commiseration for the youthful and apparently unhappy stranger.

"Young man," said he, in a softened tone, "whoever you are, or whatever may be your business here, it is my duty to have you arrested, but it would be more congenial to my feelings if you would spare me that trouble, by telling me frankly your name and intentions."

"My name can interest no one," said the man, in the same tone in which he had at first spoken, "and I have no business except to seek one who has been long lost to me."

"You speak haughtily, sir," replied the General. "Have you then no interest in making friends? Know you not that you are at this moment in my power?"

"Friends!" repeated the other with sad emphasis. "I care not for friends, since I cannot call back the lost. I am alone in this world. As to the rest I defy even the power of General Pickens!"

"Ha!" said the General, "you know me then?" and for a moment he cast his eyes in deep thought to the ground. When he looked up, the mysterious stranger was gone.

This little incident dwelt in the mind of the General. His feelings had been strangely interested by the appearance and language of the unknown; but he imagined that he must have some evil design in lurking round the fort. Why else should he be so mysterious? Perhaps he was a spy sent by some foraging party of British, who supposed that the stores of the fort might become an easy prey. At this last thought, General Pickens determined to place a stricter guard, and immediately sent out a body of men to scour the neighborhood. But they returned with the intelligence that not a single person had been found stirring within a mile of the fort.

It was a custom of General Pickens to make a circuit of the fortress every morning, to look into its welfare and attend to its little wants and necessities. At such times he had a smile and a passing word for every one.

"How goes it, Andrew, this fine morning?" he enquired of an old man, whose silver locks still curled up from the broad fair forehead, which a serene temper and healthful exercise had kept smooth and unwrinkled.

"Vera weel, yer honor," said he. "Gaid be praised for a' His mercies, and thanks to yer honor besides! Yer kind heart has been a blessin' to this country, an'--"

"Well, Andrew," interrupted the General, smiling at the grateful garrulity of the old Scotchman. "No flatteries between friends. It is the cause--the cause. The meanest soldier that fights for liberty deserves the same praise."

"Na, na, yer honor," said the old man. "It's na that ye fight for liberty sae weel, but that ye pity the puir."

"Every man should do the same," said the General. "It is bad enough fighting, but it must be worse starving. And now that I think of it, Andrew," he continued, "I would advise a stricter watch kept over this place. I must go hence to-morrow; my presence is required before Ninety-Six, and I can leave but a small garrison. You have only to keep close and be on the alert. There may be no harm meant, but I saw a very suspicious looking man prying round these walls last night, who answered me very haughtily, and refused to tell his business."

"Lord bless yer honor, what kind o' mon was he?" asked Andrew Morrison.

"He was tall and good looking as far as I could judge," said the General, "but his manner was proud and melancholy, and he disappeared very suddenly. I sent out men immediately in pursuit of him, but--"

"Heaven defend us!" exclaimed the old man in a low and rapid enunciation. "Belike it was Ralph Cornet, or aiblins his ghaist!"

The General was not superstitious, but he seemed struck with a new thought!"

"Cornet!" said he. "What! that Capt. Cornet, who rendered himself so famous among the British? I thought he was killed or drowned in this neighborhood some time ago."

"It was believed sae, yer honor," said Andrew, "but I canna

think sae. Why he was like a wild duke in the water, because, yer honor, if he gaed never sae mony times to the bottom, he aye came up alive and weel. But if the puir boy be dead, I ken weel his ghaist wad be haunting this place for--"

"You say this Cornet is a comely person?" said the General, interrupting this speech with an irrepressible smile at the old man's simplicity.

"A braw, handsome lad, as yer honor ever saw," replied the Scotchman, who was delighted at this opportunity of speaking the praise of one for whom his heart overflowed with love and pity--"yist like a young poplar, fu' sax feet high, and portly. There was nae the lad in a' the country sae strang, sae bonnie, or sae kind as the young Ralph. Wae's the day when the British blinded his young e'en wi' a sword and plume. He has been soor and mournfu' like ever since; for he had plighted his troth wi' a sonsie young leddie here, an' her father, wha has been sinking to the grund ever since the tories--fuil fa' them--brak his arm, winna hear o' the match."

"Who? the old Frenchman's daughter? Ah! I see it all now," said the General musingly.

"What is't your honor sees?" inquired Andrew respectfully.

"Why, Andrew, the man that I saw last night must have been this same Cornet, from your description. I took him for a spy. But it is likely that his ghost, as you will have it, was seeking an interview with this young lady."

"Like eneugh! like eneugh!" said the old man eagerly. "The puir boy, dead or alive, would rin a' risks to catch a glint o' her bonny e'en."

"I must look to it," said the General as he walked on.

"And sae maun I," said the Scotchman to himself. "If the puir boy hae escaped ance mair, it maunna be tauld that the bairn o' my auld freind has na ane freind in a' this land."

As the General passed on he next entered a tent in which was sitting a lady, yet in the bloom of life, whose vivacity of manner betokened a spirit which no misfortunes could conquer. She was caressing a little boy of five or six years, whose brown, curling head lay on her lap, while at her feet a little cherub girl was lying asleep.

As the happy mother looked up smiling from her babies, her radiant face afforded a striking contrast to the thin pale features of a young girl who sat not far off, with her head leaning on her hand.

"Good morning, madam," said the General, pleasantly, addressing himself to the elder lady. "Your countenance is truly agreeable in these gloomy times. It is always sunshine."

"Why, General," said she, with perfect ease and good breeding, "thanks to your care and that of the tories, I've nothing left to cry for. My husband--God bless him--is fighting in the true cause, and if I had a dozen husbands, I should wish them all so employed."

"But suppose they were all killed?" said the General, with a wondering smile.

"Then I should teach my little Willie here his duty to the British," said she, twining her fingers in the long silken curls of the pretty boy.

"Well," replied the General, "with many such mothers as you America would become another Sparta. But can't you inspire my little friend here with some of your heroism?"

"Bless you, no," said the lady, with privileged sauciness. "She is as mopish as an old owl in a hollow tree. There she has been sitting for the last half hour, poring over a lock of hair which she found by the wall, very curiously wound--into a love knot, I suppose--Heaven knows how it came there. But, General, I have been planning an excursion to amuse these sentimental young ladies."

"I should rather you would not go out," said the General. "There was a strange man prowling about here last night, and --"

As the General commenced speaking he had fixed his eyes with an expression of curiosity on Annette Bruyésant, who sat seemingly regardless of what was passing, but he stopped short, alarmed at the deep emotions his words had excited in her. The blood seemed to have forsaken her fair face, and every blue vein was plainly marked in her closed eyelids as she sank back in her seat, with her arms clasped tightly together.

Her white lips moved unconsciously, and the words, "It is he! it is he!" though murmured passionately, were rather read than heard by the General.

A frown passed over his countenance, but it was quickly succeeded by an expression of pity, and turning to the elder ady, he observed:

"I shall be obliged to leave the fort to-morrow, and I would advise you ladies to keep as close as possible during my absence."

The lady he addressed would have demurred to this, but the General asked to be admitted to the presence of old Mr. Bruyésant, who was confined to an inner part of the tent. What passed between them was never known.

General Pickens departed next morning, leaving orders with the small garrison, which remained for its protection, that no one should leave the fort except on business, and that no stranger should be admitted. But who, by arbitrary measures, ever forced a woman into a sense of her duty. Ere three days had elapsed, the gay Mrs. Cornet had rebelled against the orders of the General.

"Come, girls," said she, one fine evening "let us play them a trick! I'm sick to death of this dull place, and despite the old General and his ghost story, what say you to a little fun? Eh, Lina, what say you to a raid on the river now? Annie, I must give you a little fresh air, or a certain some one that shall be nameless will not know you when he returns from the war."

"But how shall we escape?" asked Selina Anderson, looking up listlessly from her sewing work.

"Oh, ho! leave that to me," said the lively creature, with a significant nod, as she tripped off towards the gate, where a soldier stood, true to the orders he had received. Annette and Selina were well acquainted with the mischievous tricks of this lady, but whilst they stood now wondering what she would devise to amuse the vigilance of the gate keeper, she had walked up and was screaming in the ears of the man with a tone of well affected surprise--

"Mr. Dobson, are you deaf?"

"Madam!" said the little man, staring at her in amazement.

"I say, are you deaf, that you stand here so unconcerned, when your wife has been calling you for the last half hour? Run, for pity's sake," continued she with the deepest concern, "I would not, for the world, be in your place. You know Mrs. Dobson."

"I didn't hear it, ma'am!" said poor Mr. Dobson, who first fidgeted a little uneasily, and then ran with all his speed to a tent on the opposite side of the enclosure. Besides the tories, there was nothing on earth the poor little man had so good reason to fear as his wife. The gate had been opened to fill a provision cart, which now half filled the entrance.

"Quick, quick, girls! follow me!" said the lady, who was almost dying with laughter at the success of her scheme.

In a moment more they had all glided through the opening unperceived; and the girls ran on following their gay guide, until she threw herself on the grassy bank of the river, in a perfect helplessness of mirth.

"Fie, Mrs. Cornet," said Selina Anderson gravely, "how could you be so wicked?"

"Heavens! what a little fool you are, Lina; you will never do for a warrior's wife," she replied.

Selina blushed and turned away her head.

"Bless your heart, child, don't you know 'all tricks are fair, in love and in war?' But then, poor Mr. Dobson!" she continued, "how he will fret and fume when he finds out that he has been quizzed. But no matter; if the little man is hen-pecked, sure it's not my fault. And, Willie, you are here, too, my little General," said she, on perceiving that the child had followed them. "If you don't mind we'll give you a ducking, my boy."

"You can't do it," said the child saucily. "Pa learnt me how to swim, and uncle Ralph used to throw me in the water sometimes."

"Hush, child," said his mother, in a low voice, aside to him. "Didn't I tell you not to talk of your uncle Ralph?"

"I don't care," replied the boy, with a grieved expression of countenance. "Annie Bruyésant says I may talk of him."

Annette turned deprecatingly, and took the lovely child in her arms as if to hush him; but in spite of her efforts the silent tears trickled down on his young head, to which her cheek was pressed.

With all her vivacity, Mrs. Cornet had too much real feeling not to understand and appreciate that emotion. But it was her nature to banish care, and now springing up from the bank on which she had been seated, she ordered the girls into a canoe that was lying there, and springing in herself after them, pushed it off into the stream.

A wild and frolicksome creature was that Mrs. Cornet. She cared not at what expense she followed the bent of her fancy, and all difficulties were but trifles before the vigorous impulses of her lively and independent spirit. As she sat in the stern of that little vessel and propelled its light motion by a scarcely visible effort, with those two beautiful maidens at her feet, and the little cherub boy leaning over the vessel's side, she might have passed for Amphitrite in her ocean shell. On, on, they flew, and her clear musical laugh rang over the waters like the touch of some fine instrument, redoubled and reflected in mocking silvery tones from those fancied water nymphs, the invisible echoes. At length the light bark moored itself on the point of a rock in the middle of the stream. In a moment more the delighted Mrs. Cornet had gained the flat summit of the rock, and gaily invited her less ardent companions to follow. It was, indeed, a beautiful position, and well worthy of an evening's frolic. For many miles above, the broad bosom of the river swelled on the eye, until it swept down and divided its chrystal waters against the rocky base of the island. Not a speck or stain marred the bright reflection of the pure spring-time sky. The blessed sun only was there, "careering in its fields of light," and throwing its myriads of diamond sparkles on the rippling water.

The blue rocks which covered nearly one-half the extent of the island, and dotted the stream on each side, were strewed with mosses and the lovely flowers of a thousand little twining, fibrous roots, whilst behind them rose a thicket of all that is sweet and fair in the American forest. There were the lovely jessamines and woodbines in clustering garlands over every tree and bush. The queenly flowers of the rose laurel, sitting so proudly on their emerald stems, the beautiful white acacia, and the long feathery pendants of the gray ash, with the sweet wild honey-suckle in its delicious freshness, were there, forming a wilderness such as Eden must have been in its first creation.

Mrs. Cornet felt all the wild delight of a native child of the forest newly enfranchised, and even her young companions forgot the subject of their grief for a time. The heart must be, indeed cold and callous, in which the freshness and beauty of nature cannot awaken a corresponding tone of gladness. With smiles half of pleasure and half of wonder, Annette and Selina watched the motions of their sportive guide as she leaped like a chamois over the rocks, now bending from a high point over the glassy stream, and again leaning most perilously from a bow to gather flowers. After a time she stole away unperceived, and when they looked, on hearing her gay voice, they beheld her apparently clinging to a rich garland of jessamine, which hung from the branches of a large oak, far in the midst of the island. The girls screamed involuntarily with surprise. How had she got there, unless she had the wings of a fairy?

The island was, to all appearances, perfectly unfrequented. Not a pathway, not a broken bush, not even a footstep, marked the place where any living thing had penetrated. The luxuriant canes filled up the interstices of the giant trees and flowering shrubs, rendering it all dark and inaccessible. But there she stood, with the flowers clustering around her face, which flushed with exercise and brilliant with excitement, looked the fairest flower there.

The mystery was soon explained. The trunk of a large tree had fallen across another, supporting its farthest end on the edge of the rock, and thus forming a kind of natural bridge over the tangled maze below. The young ladies proceeded along it to where Mrs. Cornet stood at its extremity; but scarcely had Annette, who was foremost, reached her, than she turned deadly pale, and her eyes seemed riveted in the glassy gaze of horror on some object before her. She would have fallen to the ground, if Mrs. Cornet had not caught her and supported her against the tree by which she was leaning.

"Lord have mercy on us!" she exclaimed. "What is the matter with the child?"

Selina Anderson, who was too much terrified to discover the cause of Annette's alarm, began to weep with affright. But the little boy, seizing his mother by the dress, exclaimed with delightful eagerness:

"La, ma! here's Rover! Ma, do look at Rover!"

Following the direction of the child's eyes, they saw a large black horse rising slowly from the ground. The canes and shrubs for a small space around him had been trodden down, and the ground was pawed into holes in many places. How he came there was a mystery; for there were no marks of ingress or egress, but a trough was fastened to a tree, where it was evident he had been fed for some time.

"Gracious, heavens! Can it indeed be Rover? What then has become of poor Ralph? Or maybe he is about here," said Mrs. Cornet, looking round a little wildly.

At the mention of that name so fraught with terrible remembrance, an undefined awe seized the minds of the adventurous females. They clung closer together, seeming for the first time to feel alone in that unfrequented place.

"Let us go from here," whispered Annette faintly.

But before they turned to depart, Mrs. Cornet, to assure herself that it was indeed the horse of her husband's ill-fated brother, called him by name, and the animal, familiar to the sound of her voice, walked up to her and evinced his recognition of her by many mute but intelligible signs of joy.

Amusing spirit seemed to have seized Mrs. Cornet. She left her store of gathered flowers to wither on the rock, and resumed her station in the canoe in silence. At length she said, almost unconsciously:

"If Ralph Cornet is about here we shall soon see him. But then," she continued, "the horse seems to have been a long time on the island."

For the first time in her life she appeared to be puzzled, and she said no more.

A sigh from Annette was the only answer she received. That speech had aroused the poor girl from similar thoughts. They returned in perfect silence to the fort, for Selina Anderson had not sufficiently recovered from her fright to be conversable, and the little boy had cried himself to sleep on his mother's lap at the thought of leaving his favorite Rover behind.

Mr. Dobson, the much abused gate keeper, whose goodness merited better treatment than he received, admitted them with perfect good humor; for he had learnt a very sad lesson of forced submission to a woman. But the little man resolved in his inmost heart to be fast enough for them next time.

CHAPTER VII

"How dear the dream in darkest hour of ill,
Should all be changed, to find thee faithful still;
Be but thy heart like Selim's firmly shown,
To thee be Selim's tender as thine own,
To soothe each sorrow, share in each delight,
Blend every thought--do all but disunite."

IT had become a settled conviction in the mind of Annette that Ralph Cornet was still living. In the lock of hair found within the wall, she recognized some of her own which had once been in his possession, and this circumstance, connected with the words which General Pickens had spoken in her presence, confirmed in her the suspicion that Ralph had employed this as a certain and plain telegraph to her heart. The discovery of his horse awakened her to the keenest and most distressing suspense. The reflection that he was in the neighborhood, and obliged to conceal himself in the midst of dangers, was rendered still bitterer by the thought that he had not a single being on whom to rely for comfort; for his father had been killed by the tories long since. In this desolate situation, she, too, had apparently deserted him; and the affectionate girl felt that it would be some consolation if she could only see him and assure him of the violence her coldness had done to her feelings. But after that wild sally from the fort, the garrison was proof against the stratagems or entreaties of the ladies, and Annette despaired of seeing the object of her solicitude.

Fate was, however, accomplishing her wishes by the severest test of her affections. In a few weeks a funeral procession emerged from the fort, and Annette followed as chief mourner that humble coffin. Her father had never recovered from his first attack. Besides the wound in his arm he had received an injury in the chest, which brought on a pulmonary affection, and he declined gradually--so gradually that no alarm was conveyed to the heart of Annette until near the last moments.

Nearly the whole garrison followed the remains of Pierre Bruyésant, that humble but devout supporter of truth and liberty, to the grave. He was buried, according to his own request, under an elm tree near his cottage. The last sod was replaced over the spot where the grassy turf had been disturbed, and the procession moved back to the fort; but Annette could not be torn away.

"Leave me for a moment alone with him," she begged, and there were none hard hearted enough to refuse that sacred request. When they had all gone, Annette threw herself on the newly made grave, in that agony of a young spirit when first it feels alone and desolate. In all the world she knew not of one being who shared the blood of her veins.

--"None that with kindred consciousness endued, If she were not, would seem to smile the less."

And she sobbed aloud the endearing name of father, in the despairing accents of the shipwrecked mariner who sees his last hope, the shattered plank on which he had borne himself, sink down beneath the wave. How long she remained thus insensible to all but the weight of her afflictions, she knew not, nor was she aware that the child of Mrs. Cornet had lingered with a kindly instinct near her, until he clung to her, screaming with affright.

Aroused by the cries of the child, Annette raised herself, and as she looked up she saw the object of her alarm in a man who was standing within three feet of them. It was Ralph Cornet, but so pale, so wan, so different from his former self, that it was no wonder the little boy did not recognize him. He was dressed plainly in a suit of dark cloth, which rendered almost ghostly the expression of his pale, sad countenance, and a frightful scar extended over his left eyebrow.

The surprise, the shock of his appearance, was too much for the weakened nerves of the poor girl, and she would have fallen again to the ground if she had not been caught in the arms of her lover. How wildly did he call upon her to look upon him once more--and how passionately did he kiss the pale face which hung like a drooping flower on his arm! But the warm blood soon flowed back in fitful gushes to her cheek, and her eyes opened upon him; but she did not this time withdraw herself from his embrace. Her mind was impaired by grief and long suffering--she had no more the power of resistance; and besides, in the heart-weary loneliness of her situation, she felt that the breast on which she leaned was the only link that bound her to the dear memories of the past. Who so well could sympathize with her in her joy's decline as he who by the sweet enchantment of his presence had given them their gladness? But while Annette, with woman's natural faithfulness to her hallowed memories, fondly reflected on the past, Ralph Cornet thought only of the future; and as he recounted to her the series of misfortunes which had befallen him, while her head rested quietly on his shoulder, he felt "the rapture which kindles out of woe."

The tones of his voice were like a delicious strain of music to Annette--music long and well remembered. It is true they had lost the lingering joyousness of other and better days, but they had now the subdued and yearning tenderness which sorrow wrings from the heart. Strange it is that its pure worth is never known until tried in the fire of affliction! The gay know not the wealth of their affections, or the touching softness, the fervor, the fidelity which spring up from the bruised heart; for passion is the rebel offspring of disappointment.

"And now, my darling Annie," continued Ralph Cornet--in a voice which came, 'o'er her ear like the sweet South wind which breathes upon a bank of violets'--"we are alone in this world; why should we be separated more? It is true, as you foretold me, I am a dishonored man, feared and despised by my countrymen. Yet for all that I care not, since you do not hate me! It has been the consequence of my early errors, and I am not a man to weep idly over what is past. But, my own love, though there is no longer a place of peace and safety for us here, we need not despair. In the distant regions of the far West, I have heard them say there are lands richer far than this, and spots more beautiful, where the Indian lives all the year round without toil or trouble, with his feathery bow and his lowing herds. There, by some pretty stream, we will build a little cottage which shall remind us of this, and there we will be all the world to each other." Annette wept on in silence. Her griefs were too fresh and strong, and disappointment had weighed too heavily on her mind for her to be able yet to realise the bright creations of this day-dream.

Ralph, who in the elastic buoyancy which love had imparted to his mind, felt the springing hopes which he so vividly pictured, seemed hurt that she did not participate in them.

"You do not speak, Annette; you do not say that you will go with me," said he, mournfully. "Surely I have not deceived myself in the dear hope that when the world grew dark around me, and every face was averted from me, there would be one heart unchanged, one smile, which shining as a beacon of hope, would lead me back to the peace and happiness I had lost."

Annette raised her head and looked up in his face. The flush which excitement had brought into his cheeks, was fading away before the deeply mournful expression of his thoughts, and she felt pained at the memory of all her coldness must have wrought on his sensitive soul.

"Ralph Cornet, you have sworn never more to take up arms against your country?" she asked eagerly.

"Never, my love, so help me God, except in my own defence!" he replied.

"Then," said she, "here on this sacred altar, I renew my former vow to be unto you what I have ever been, true in heart; to leave all, yes, even this precious spot of earth, to follow--"

Sobs choked her utterance, and as the young man knelt and folded his arms around her, tears came into his own eyes--tears of sublime emotion.

"It is enough," he whispered. "My own love. You are what I always thought you, the truest and best of womankind. It is true I once feared that you had permitted those around you to estrange your affections from me. But forgive me, love--I suffered enough for that thought." Ralph went on again to picture the bright hopes which he had imagined of an elysium in another land, where malice and treachery could not reach them, and where without any law but nature, or other guide than love, they should enjoy the ease and happiness of the primitive inhabitants of earth.

"Why should we wait any longer?" said he. "We have nothing left to bind us to this spot."

A blush crimsoned over Annette's pale features, and she

answered, hesitatingly--

"But, Ralph, I cannot go except as--as your wife."

"I, too, I have thought of that, my love," said he, smiling fondly. "I saw Andrew Morrison this morning, who informed me that he would be here on this mournful occasion. Something whispered me that you would be true, and the plan which I have just revealed to you of leaving the country, then occurred to me. There is in the fort with you a French minister, a good and kind man, who, for the love he bore your father, might be prevailed on to do us this service. I will engage Andrew to bring him here--even to-morrow night, if you--"

"What, so soon Ralph? And my poor father just buried to-day!" And Annette burst into a fresh passion of tears.

"My beloved Annie, do not grieve so--you shall have it as you please. But I am becoming very cowardly since you have rendered life so dear to me; and there is no safety for me here."

"Well, Ralph, well," said Annette resignedly. "But I must return to the fort; and how shall I escape again?"

"Why return, my love! I can place you in safety until to-morrow, and then I shall bid them defiance forever."

"No, no!" said Annette, who was becoming alarmed for his safety, "that must not be. My absence from the fort would excite suspicion--they would search for us, and then all would be lost."

"Do not fear, Annette," said Ralph, smiling at her earnestness. "No power on earth shall tear you from me now. But return to the fort as you have prudently suggested. Andrew Morrison is my friend--you may depend upon him--and I will be ready with a rope ladder on the western side of the fort, to receive you. Here, where we have enjoyed so many years of happiness, we will be wedded; and then we will bid farewell forever to all that can remind us of sorrow."

The little boy, who was alarmed at the first sight of Ralph, had been sitting at their feet listening with perplexed interest to this conversation; but by this time he seemed to recognise him, and clasping him by the knees, he said:

"And I will go, too! May I not go, uncle Ralph?"

Ralph had left him hitherto unnoticed, but he now sat him on his knee and caressed him fondly.

"No, Willie, no!" said he, "you must stay to take care of your mother."

The child was not insensible to these caresses, and he threw his arms around his uncle's neck, as he was wont to do-- "Where have you been gone so long, uncle Ralph? Annie Bruyésant has cried so much for you," said he, in infantile simplicity.

"But Annie Bruyésant will cry no more now," said Ralph, with a smile, whilst putting aside the curls to kiss the brow of his little relative.

Willie made no reply. His attention seemed to be fixed on something opposite to him. They were very near the deserted cottage, which, since it had been rifled by the tories, stood with its doors open or broken down--

"Look, uncle Ralph, look!" said he. "Yonder is a man peeping through the door!"

Ralph looked up hastily.

"Oh, no, Willie, you are mistaken," said he.

But the child would not be satisfied till Ralph went with him to search the house. There was no one visible. Annette, however, had become alarmed, and after a few more whispered words she took the hand of the little boy and returned with trembling steps to the fort. Ralph Cornet waited until the last glimpse of her form was hid from his sight by the thick trees, and then he turned away also.

CHAPTER VIII

"Ambition is at distance
A goodly prospect, tempting to the view.
The height delights us, and the mountain top
Looks beautiful, because 'tis nigh to heaven.
But we ne'er think how sandy's the foundation--
What storms will batter, and what tempests shake it."

IN the meantime the British officer had been fulfilling a wild and bitter destiny. When on that eventful morning he fled before his pursuers to the river, he found that he had but one resource. The pursuers were close at hand, and he could not have reached the other bank in safety if even his wound had not incapacitated him from swimming. But from a boy he had acquired great proficiency in the sport of diving, and was noted for the length of time he could remain under the water. Ralph now turned this talent to good account. With his handkerchief he first bound tightly the orifice where a bullet had entered his thigh, and jumping into the water, he contrived, by swimming and diving, to reach a place where its transparency would least betray him, and where a body of leaves had drifted up against an old log which extended far into the river, where he concealed himself with just enough of his face above the water to insure respiration through the friendly covering of the leaves. When his enemies reached the bank he heard the curses of disappointment, the dreadful imprecations uttered against him; but deeper than the bitterness of all this was the sickening feeling of contempt with which he discovered the treachery of Hugh Bates.

"And it is with such men that I am classed!" he said to himself, as he lay all day under that close watch. Nature was nearly exhausted; but Ralph Cornet would sooner have given himself as food to the fishes than to have become the prize of those desperate men. But when the electric waters conveyed to him the last echoes of their retreating footsteps, he raised himself and looked around.

The moon was riding high on a sky of that soft exquisite blue which belongs purely to the American autumn, and as its bright rays fell upon the river, seemingly setting the liquid element on fire with a flood of silver light, it appeared as if a new heaven and earth were created within that immense reflection. The bright yellow and red tints of the autumnal trees, mingling with the fadeless hues of the majestic evergreens on the western bank, lay mirrored there in a dream-like repose, which the stillness of night and the deeply contrasting shades around rendered almost fearful. Ralph gazed a few moments; but in those few moments what years of agonised thought were comprised! Not that he had never viewed that scene before. He had looked on nature in all her varied and beautiful forms, and held communion from his infancy with river, rock and hill. He was nature's foster child. From her whispered teachings he had gleaned all the knowledge he possessed, and in the days of his innocence he had loved her voice. But now, from the depths of that awful volume, a tone went to his heart, which for the first time, awakened remorse. He felt that he was not what he had been; that he never could be that free, that happy, that joyous thing again.

As a sense of his utter wretchedness, of his degradation came over him, the illusions which had dazzled his youthful imagination faded away and revealed to him the meagre skeleton he had embraced. Hunted like a wild beast by the best part of his countrymen, betrayed by the other, with whom his spirit seemed to mingle--and she, even she had deserted him.

Oppressed by all these thoughts, faint from loss of blood, and benumbed with cold, Ralph Cornet sank on the ground. This man of pride, and strength, and daring, now that there was nothing left to live for, resolved to die there alone and in darkness. Cold shivering fits came over him, succeeded by a feeling of suffocating heat which brought the cold perspiration to his brow, and soon he would have been in a raging fever, but that guardian angel which guides the children of mercy through storm and darkness whispered a word of hope which drew the wretched man from the verge of despair.

"There is yet one being left to pity me," said he. "I will arise and go to my father. I have wronged him, but he will pardon me." He arose and followed the thickety bank for some miles, insensible alike to pain, fear or danger. But the cool air and exercise moderated the excitement of his blood, and his senses gradually became clearer. He had arrived within a mile of his home when he heard the splashing of oars in the water. Every stroke of the paddles became fainter, and he stooped down to the bank just in time to observe a party of four or five men landing on the Georgia side from the kind of canoe then commonly in use.

"What can these rascally Doolys have been after?" thought he. "They are no friends to our family!" and Ralph's step quickened involuntarily as he thought of his father's lonely and unprotected situation.

His worst fears were confirmed, for the first sight which greeted him was a column of black smoke streaked with fitful gushes of red flame rising from his native dwelling. He gave not one glance to the ruin around him, but rushed into the house, calling loudly on the name of his father. His voice was lost in the loud roaring of the devouring element; but by the horrid glare which overspread the room, he recognized a bed in one corner, from which hung the body of a human being, as if it had fallen in the attempt to escape. Ralph Cornet staid not to assure himself that it was his father. He staggered forward, and seizing the body bore it from the devouring flames. He laid it upon the grass in the bright moonlight, and threw himself upon it in bitter anguish; but scarcely had he done so, when he started up suddenly, exclaiming:

"Oh, God! he lives!" And placing the head upon his knee, he put back the silvery hair from the high, pale brow. The blood began to stream afresh from a wound in the shoulder as the fresh air revived him, and Ralph observed that a bullet had passed quite through it, causing a great effusion of blood, which, independent of the suffocating effects of the burning house, would have occasioned a swoon. The young man shuddered at the thought that but a few minutes later and he would have seen only the ashes of his father's funeral pyre. But as he reflected that a good angel had guided him there for the purpose of saving his father's life, he felt that he was not quite a wretch. With something of joyful alacrity he bound up the wound, and seeing his father's lips move at the pain which the action occasioned, Ralph bent his ear close to catch the sound.

"Begone!" said the old man, faintly. "Let me die in peace!"

"Father!" said Ralph fondly, "you may yet live."

The father's eyes opened. "James, is it you, my son?" he asked.

"No, father, it is your poor Ralph."

The red glow of the flames threw a vivid light upon that spot, and the old man looked up long and earnestly in the pale countenance that was bending over him. His own was not more ghastly. As if slowly recollecting something painful, his brow gathered into a dark frown, and he made an impatient gesture with his hand.

"Go, go!" said he. "I cannot bear you."

"Father!" said Ralph, in an agony of imploring tenderness, "surely you do not hate me too?"

"Yes, I hate you," replied he in a hollow and shivering tone of wrath. "I hate you as much as I ever loved you before. You were my darling, my youngest born--the last gift of your mother who is above. In all this country there was none like you. I saw in you the glory of my own youth revived, and I prided in you. But you have disgraced--you have humbled me. You are the first traitor of my blood!" And, exhausted by this torrent of passion, the old man sunk back, with his head on the grass, and gnashed his teeth in anguish.

"Take back the word--take back the word!" said Ralph. "I have betrayed no trust!"

"Boy!" said the old man, raising himself with a violent gesture, and pointing with one hand to the house, the timbers of which had just fallen in with a loud crash, and sent up a strong lurid flame to the sky. "Boy, behold your work! Freedom, freedom was your trust, and behold one of her many pillars fallen through your means. You first neglected and then raised your own arm against her. Call you not that treason?"

"Oh, God!" said Ralph. "Must I bear all this?"

The last drop of his cup was full. His heart was humbled as a child's, and he burst into tears.

The proud father turned suddenly to him, as if doubtful of what he heard, and as he regarded him a few moments, the ferocity which gleamed in his eyes subsided into a calm and concentrated gaze of contempt, the strong impulsive bitterness of which convulsed his features with a ghastly and unconscious smile.

"Miserable boy!" said he. "What has become of the strength of your glorious patriotism? Traitors, at least, should never weep. They should have that one virtue--the power to bear. Go; you are not of my blood. I disown you!"

"Father!" said Ralph fiercely, "cease your reproaches. Whatever may have been my early errors, I have wept for them in tears of blood."

"Then why not redeem them, boy?"

"And act a double treason!" said Ralph. "No! I will die in the faith I have sworn."

"Then leave me," said the old man. "Leave me forever!"

"Not 'til I have placed you in safety, father!" said Ralph, mournfully. "The tories will return to see if their work prospers, and they must not find you here."

"And is it you who would protect me against the tories?" said the father sneeringly.

Ralph bit his lips until the blood gushed from them. But without trusting himself to reply, he seized the feeble frame of the old man in his arms and tottered with it to the brink of the river. A canoe was quietly playing there in an eddy of the stream--Ralph's own canoe--the bark of his boyish sallies! Somehow, amid all the changes that had passed, it had been spared. Perhaps, like modest worth, it could flatter no passion, serve no interest.

Just as he had left it it remained, locked to a willow. The key was lost, but Ralph wrenched away the pin, and placed his father in it, and having given one last look to the painful scene behind him, where the fiery streaks were fading away on the horizon, he breathed a bitter curse on those who had wrought this destruction of household wealth, this utter desolation, and then guided his little canoe swiftly and noiselessly down the stream. He remembered a hanging rock, beneath which he had once taken shelter from a storm on the river. It was a retired place, completely hid by the rising ground and trees, and only accessible by means of a lagoon which backed up from the river. The eye of mortal man seldom visited the spot; indeed, it was so entirely hemmed in by the swampy verdue of the two hills which enclosed it, and was besides so dark and gloomy that it offered but little to tempt the curiosity or daring of the boldest. But where was it Ralph Cornet had not penetrated? There was not a single creek or inlet, for many miles along that river, which he had not explored in his indulged and adventurous childhood, and every dell and cave had opened its secret treasures to his eye; for, as the heir of an independent estate, his aristocratic father had fostered in him the bold and daring spirit which led him to rove unshackled through nature's wide domain, and perfect himself in all the hardy branches of her science, rather than submit to the dull training of domestic labor. This the father had never regretted until now; for though his proud boy had the strongest arm, and the lightest and merriest heart in the whole country, there were none more passionately fond, more considerately kind. Even his wild, ungoverned passions had a tone so generous and elevated that every one predicted that young Cornet would be a blessing to his country. His father listened, and wound him still more closely around his heart. When the time came that his eldest son volunteered for the service of the State, though he saw the fire of ardor burning in Ralph's eye, he could not resolve to give him up. How different would have been his course if he could have foreseen that in so short a time the self-governed spirit of the youth would betray the imperfections of his judgment to his ruin.

Now he was "fallen, fallen, fallen from his high estate," and the dregs of that father's immeasurable love were stirred into anguish not unmingled with remorse, but the pride which had so qualified that affection, now in its mistified bitterness, deceived the old man into the belief that he really felt the hatred he expressed for his son. Yet in that moment Ralph Cornet would have died to save his father! He understood by nature's sympathy how the strength of his love betrayed itself in the violence of his hatred, and as an atonement for its justice, which he felt, he resolved to devote himself with humble and filial duty to his protection. Ralph well knew the unsleeping vigilance, the untiring wolf-like ferocity of his father's enemies. He hardly thought of his own perilous situation, but he conducted his light canoe, freighted with the almost insensible body of his father, to the wild spot before mentioned, as the only place of refuge for them both. The moon was sinking behind the western bank of the river, but it threw its last ray obliquely into that gloomy retreat, and by its light Ralph gathered a couch of dried leaves under the rock, and laid his father upon it. He also took off his coat--that coat lately so fine with the trappings and badges of his relations with the royalists, but now tarnished sadly by the day's misfortunes--and formed a pillow for the haughty republican's head.

For many days and nights Ralph watched him there in secret, and his tender assiduities, his untiring patience through the reproaches and fretfulness of sickness and anger, at length won nature back to his father's heart.

"Bless you, bless you, my boy!" said he one morning when Ralph, having returned with fresh water and dressed his wound, placed some food before him. "Surely such a kind heart as yours must be brave and noble, however it may have been duped. But how pale you look, my son! I fear confinement in this horried place will kill you. Better you had left me to be burnt alive, for those rascals will have me at last. They can never rest since that unfortunate shot with which I killed their brother as he was carrying off my English mare. The thieving dog! he was paid for it."

"No, father," said Ralph. "You are safe here for a time, I trust. No one but old Juba knows of our existence, and he is not likely to betray us. We can remain here until these troublesome times are over, for, sure as there is a God above, our wretched country will rise sometime from under the rule of the wicked."

"That's spoken like my son," said the old man, with a fond and almost cheerful accent.

That day, contrary to his usual custom--for he only ventured out in the darkest hour of night--Ralph rowed his canoe for some distance up the steep and narrow gorge of the lagoon until he found a place where he might land. As he clambered up the bank the branch of the tree to which he had clung broke off and fell into the stream, but he heeded not the circumstance, and having gained the summit, he took a circuitous route across the woods to the hut of the old

African, from whom he had hitherto received the supplies which sustained his father and himself in their exile. This old negro had long been supported by his father for the good he had done, and though he now lived to himself, and was actually free, he gloried in the relation of master and servant, and still retained the warm affection for his master's family which time had strengthened into a habit in his faithful nature. He would sooner have been flayed alive than have betrayed them, and cheerfully shared with them the daily pittance which he either earned or begged, for he had saved but little from his master's stores. It was a lonely, long and unfrequented way which Ralph had to traverse, and the sun was setting at evening, when he again entered his canoe. As the little vessel heaved up and settled its point upon the sand, Ralph was alarmed by the sight of many footsteps and marks of violence, and rushing into the cave he fell on his knees before the horrid spectacle of his father's bloody and mangled corpse. Wildly he raised the head to assure himself that life was indeed gone, and that he was all alone. Then his brain seemed to whirl round, and he held his brow with a maddening clasp, until tears came to his relief.

During the night he scooped a shallow grave under the rock where, without other shroud than his tattered garments, he laid the violated remains of his deeply loved parent. The tears which he had at first shed relieved the weight on his heart, for they were lightened by the reflection that he had soothed the sufferings of that parent, and that his last words had been a blessing. Perhaps, too, he consoled himself that those eyes were closed on a world where they would have seen only sorrow. But that awful burial of the murdered--there, alone, and in darkness, was an outrage too shocking to the feelings of a son, and as he proceeded in the bitter task the tears became congealed on his eyelids, and a stern rancor poured over the latent softness of his heart. He went forth from that cave harsh and unpitying as a savage, vowing to match the blood of a Dooly with that so freely shed.

The old man had spoken truly from an intimate knowledge of the character of these fierce men. They could not rest while they thought their brother's blood cried to them from the ground, and when they had shot his destroyer in his bed, and set fire to the house over his head, after having secured to themselves everything valuable, they believed their revenge consummated. It was generally supposed that old Cornet had perished thus, and they had no suspicion of the fact of his escape, until as they were passing down the river the fated morning of Ralph's absence, a green branch floating on the mouth of the lagoon excited their curiosity so far as to lead them to investigate the mystery. As the man who believed he had killed some poisonous reptile, and seeing it again move its fangs, springs upon it, and ends not until he has crushed it from the form of nature, thus they sprung upon that weak old man, and mangled him with wanton and beastly cruelty. But, as if in confirmation of the truth that "murder will out," they left by mistake a gun behind them, which they had stolen from his father, and by this means Ralph, if he had doubted it before, would have been able to identify the murderers.

They would doubtless return soon to look for it; at least Ralph judged so, and he lingered there with the hope that they would come, that he might on that spot satisfy the manes of his father. But towards daylight he grew impatient and left the cave. A new and fierce ambition had seized him; it was the desire of drowning his sorrows in the noise of battle--of revenging on his kind some of the misery which maddened him. He had now no ties for good or evil; but he remembered the friendship of Ferguson, who had not appeared ungrateful for the assistance he had rendered him, and he resolved if possible to join him in his operations as he originally intended, and resume command of a company which he had undesignedly relinquished. It was, as I have said, near daylight when Ralph Cornet, without scrip or staff, except the gun which had been left by the rock, boldly began his journey.

He took no secret turns, no winding ways, to avoid detection, for his heart was filled with a strange longing, a thirst for human blood; and he watched eagerly for his enemies, but no creature crossed his path. It happened, however, that his route lay near the old African's dwelling; and as he was passing within half a mile of it, his attention was aroused by screams, or rather by sounds which appeared to be the involuntary and irrepressible outpourings of agony. His heart smote him with having forgotten that humble friend, and he quickened his steps in that direction. As he approached, the sound of a lash was distinctly heard, and occasionally laughter and curses contrasted mockingly with the scream which attended each stroke. Ralph stood by a tree outside the little enclosure of corn and potatoes which surrounded the hut, whence he had a plain view of the scene, which made his blood to boil once more. There was his faithful Juba, hanging by the arms from a log which extended from a corner of the hut, and a man was still inflicting the punishment of the whip, accompanying every stripe with an injunction and threat about something which the old negro refused to reveal, the nature of which Ralph could not at first determine. Two other men stood by with drawn swords, laughing fiendishly at the manner in which the negro winced from the cruel torture of their companion; but every now and then, enraged at his stubborn silence, they ran up and thrust the points of their swords into his flesh, or seized him by the short kinks of grey hair, threatening to flay him alive if he did not tell them where Ralph Cornet was at that moment. The blood of the African streamed over his ebon skin, but no expostulation or entreaty escaped him. His white eyes rolled disdainfully upon them, and his thick lips were closed in perfect silence. He refused to utter a single word. Ralph heard all that passed, and unable to contain himself any longer he examined the priming of the rifle and resting it slowly and steadily against the tree he took deliberate aim at the man who held the lash, for as he had once turned round and discovered his face the dark joy of revenge rose in the breast of Ralph. With the report of the gun the man sprang at least three feet into the air, and fell, like a lump of lead, with a groan. His companions, so taken by surprise, jumped over the fence and fled as if a legion had been at their heels. Ralph staid only to release the negro, and whispered "farewell!" The morning sun rose on him many miles distant.

It was the third day of his travel that somewhat exhausted with so many miles journeying on foot, and almost without food or sleep, he sat down to rest by a little mountain stream near the border of North Carolina. He knew not what to think, for the last night and day he had met parties of men, some of whom seemed to be flying either on horse or foot, and others pursuing. Neither party had any marks by which he could distinguish friend or foe; for, knowing that the soiled British uniform which he still wore would render him liable to suspicion, he kept at a distance. But he judged that some army had been routed, and he feared much for Ferguson from whom he had as yet received no information.

As he sat with his arms folded on his breast revolving these thoughts, a man approached him on foot who appeared also to be a traveler. He stood for some time regarding Ralph with an expression of much curiosity, who, when he had lifted up his head, testified no less surprise and emotion in discovering him to have been once a member of his own company of militia. The fugitive soldier sat down there and told the story to his newly-arisen Captain of their conflicts with the mountaineers--of the death of the valiant Ferguson--and of the total rout and capture of his army. Ralph listened in silence to this relation which brought annihilation to his hopes and destruction to his day-dream of glory. But when the man went on to state that Ferguson, on report of his death, had given his horse to the new Captain who headed his company, and that this man together with the horse were now with a part of the other prisoners remaining not far off, Ralph started to his feet and shouted as if that cry had sounded in the ears of an army instead of the lone woods---

"To the rescue!--to the rescue!"

The soldier, who had a brother among the prisoners, eagerly entered into the bold design of Ralph, which was to rally the flying royalists--of whom he felt assured there were yet many wandering on the mountains--and endeavor to recover the prisoners by surprise.

The attempt succeeded beyond his expectation, for he soon found himself at the head of twenty or thirty men, wild, desperate, daring tories, who knowing that their lives were already staked on the no longer doubtful contest with their countrymen, threw themselves recklessly into the adventure.

Under the limb of a large tree, near to what appeared to be an American encampment, a rude scaffolding was erected, around which were bustling many men in lively preparation for some uncommon event. All seemed to be ready for moving when this should have been accomplished. There were no signs of tents or baggage wagons, but arms and knapsacks lay about in heaps, and several fires were yet smoking. To the left a number of horses, ready equipped, were tied to the dwarfish shrubs, whilst between them and the scaffold sat or reclined that part of the captured royalists which had been committed to the care of Colonel Shelby, bound and secured by means of chains to the trees.

These had been detained some few days after the departure of the rest by the indisposition of the officer, and their captors, without fear of molestation, were making ready to offer offended justice an expiation for the blood of many innocent victims. From the ranks of the prisoners, one after another, a man was loosed and hung from the limbs of the tree; and it was not the first time that the Whigs were provoked to that method of retaliation. But whilst these executions were going on, amid laughing and shouting, which mocked the screams of the victims, a noise was heard behind, and it was observed that the remaining captives were loosed and running down the hill in the rear. There was swift snatching of arms and mounting of horses, and the last victim, with the cord yet unbound around his neck, was left alone. But in the meantime Ralph Cornet, with the eye of a lynx had espied his horse among those ready bridled and saddled, and having slyly loosed and mounted him, he warmly met and charged the pursuers in front of the better half of his men, in the deep copse-wood of the valley. The mountaineers pressed on furiously, but Ralph covered the retreat of the prisoners to a rude defense he had thrown up in one of the fastnesses of the mountains, and the retreating fire he kept up obliged the pursuers, who had set off hastily and without order, to return and rally their forces.

The situation which Ralph had chosen was perfectly secure from attack, and he might have maintained his position there for any length of time, if famine had not obliged him to abandon it. He knew that Colonel Shelby, strongly reinforced, was watching them, and under these circumstances he found it necessary to make a push for the lower country. They sallied out one night, but they had not proceeded far when they were attacked in the rear. This was what they had expected, and each man by the light of the clear, cold starlight, turned and grappled with his foe. The conflict was stern and desperate, but not long. The numbers were now unequal, not more than half of the tories had arms, and every man but Ralph was either killed or captured. When his last comrade fell fighting by his side, Ralph Cornet, who was himself stunned by a blow on the head, turned and fled. For a long time he imagined he heard the tramp of feet behind him, but when at dawn of day he pulled up his good horse to breathe, on the top of a high hill, he looked around, and he was alone. A wide landscape stretched out to the west in successive variation of undulating slopes, over which the blue mists of morning spread a soft and hallowed repose. The wearied and misanthropic spirit of Ralph yearned towards its still and apparently untrodden solitude. He gazed back for a moment to the gentle vales of the South--

"My country!" he said aloud, "it is in vain that we struggle. You will be free--but I--I cannot see it!"

And plunging down the hill, he was soon threading the lovely vales of the Toogula. But all was too soft and beautiful there to sympathise with the harsh tenor of his thoughts. He sought for the stern and terrible, that he might hide from himself in the subduing presence of that nature which had ever been his god. At length the dark-green mountain tops rose above him, and scarcely less than a madman, he wandered by the "beetling brows" of precipices, and through the gloomy grave-like hollows. His horse fed beside him on the green verdure of the sheltered spots; but it was many, many days that Ralph Cornet forgot the cravings of nature except to snatch instinctively the wild grapes and berries that hung to his hand. No sign of human habitation was there, and only once an Indian hunter had crossed his path, casting on him a sly inquiring glance. The wolves howled around where he struck his fire of nights, and not unfrequently a bear ran off at sight of him. He still carried his gun, and the leathern pouch on his shoulder had some few charges of ammunition remaining. But the wild deer played around him unharmed, and watched him with their timid eyes in wondering innocence.

One day he found himself on the edge of a rock where a little stream, swollen by the autumnal rains, came rushing down from the dark brow of the mountain, through rustling leaves and chiming cascades, and he nearly precipitated himself over the brink before he was aware of the gulf that yawned beneath him. Then, suddenly as the lightning scathes the living tree, the full sublimity of that mountain cataract ran through the nerves of Ralph. He fell prostrate on the rock, and gazed down into the yawning abyss and drank in the roaring of the waters, until his strained eyes ached almost to bursting, and his brain whirled round with ecstasy. Scarcely could he refrain from throwing himself headlong, in sympathy with the torrent, down, down into its eddying pool--so fascinating, so impelling to his soul were these elements of the beautiful and terrible.

Long, very long, he gazed, and then winding around to the foot of the mountain, he entered the amphitheatre of the precipice, and seating himself by the circular pool, looked up nearly two hundred feet to where the water poured over the rim of the rock. His mind was over wrought by the novel excitement, and he laughed loud and exultingly as the strong breeze brushed the hair from his brow and the cool spray dashed in his face.

"Ha! ha! ha!" he shouted, "these are my companions!" And he stooped down and kissed the rocks, and shouted again, and clapped his hands in the ecstasy of insanity.

It was a fearful moment; for he was about to plunge into the dark and unfathomed basin of the torrent. But a stream of lightning, for several seconds in succession, blinded his eyes and a clap of thunder broke on the rock so vividly that, pained by the shock, he sunk down on the ground, with his head buried in his arms. A silence succeeded of such long continuance that Ralph ventured to look up, and his eyes caught the inky surges heaving like the waters of a boiling cauldron on the sky. Presently he heard a low rumbling, like a thousand chariot wheels afar off, and the wind whistled shrilly through the dry leaves of the forest above him. But soon after the discharge, as of a cannonade, rattled through the hollows in reverberating peals, and the winds lashed the sides of the mountain, and roared and swelled, until the hoary trees on the mountain's brow tossed their arms in distraction, and groaned and creaked as their trunks were twisted off and hurled like leaves through the air. Ralph threw himself on the ground and prepared to die, in trembling terror; for man, though he dares to defy his Maker, shrinks from an exhibition of His Almighty power. But the war of elements passed on--the rain ceased, and subdued by the voice of Him who speaketh to the tempest, Ralph Cornet's madness departed and he fell on his knees and gave thanks for a life preserved. He had returned to himself and felt his wretchedness; but he went forth an humble and a reasonable man. The spirit of murmuring was quelled, and his mind was strengthened in its sadness. Impelled by hunger, he sought and obtained food, and then wandered farther into the heart of the mountains; for the poetry of his nature was breathing out after their beautiful mysteries.

Ere long, of necessity, he came upon the rich shadows of Tallulah, garnered up there in the wild depths of the forest as a thing too precious for the eye of man to profane, where lights and shades, and colors were blended so harmoniously and so gracefully with all that is mighty and terrible in magnificence, and all appearing as new and fresh and beautiful as if an admiring God, enchanted of his work, had exempted it from his decree against a fallen world. It burst a glorious vision on the eyes of Ralph, as if a scroll of darkness and error had been suddenly withdrawn from his mind, and the happy buoyancy of his dreaming time harmonized with the soft brilliancy of the scene.

For weeks he wandered along those lonely cliffs, which for many miles enclose that chrystal rivulet into the sweetest prison house that nature ever formed. Sometimes he would stand for hours gazing from the dizzy heights, and then he would descend perilously a thousand feet down into the chasm, and look nearer on those painted walls, where they lost themselves in the forest trees just a little below the sky, until he drank his fill of beauty. He was there alone amid the grandeur of nature, with no evidence before him of fallen man--no wonder that he forgot the curse of his being. His heart was softened, his mind purified and exalted by the mysterious process of assimilating to God through his works, and he began again, as in the days of his innocence, to weave sweet dreams of intercourse with his kind. One morning, in a fit of musing, he turned his horse's head, almost involuntarily, towards his once happy home.

Ralph did not deceive himself with regard to the danger of returning again to the haunts of men. He hoped that the rancor of his enemies was somewhat abated by his long absence, but he could only expect forgiveness from one. To her his heart yearned the more tenderly, because her image was connected with the only things pleasant in his bitter memory, and was, beneath the sky, the only light that shone on his darkened spirit. He was riding along leisurely through the scenes which reminded him of all he had hoped and lost in the course of one year, when a man passed by him at full gallop, but he thought no more of the circumstance, and had arrived safely near the river, indulging in a strange sweet reverie--very strange for one who was approaching his country without a place to lay his head. But he was thinking of her, that soft and loving being who had been always ready to excuse his errors since childhood. It is true she had, at their last dreadful meeting, appeared cold, and that coldness had nerved his heart for deeds of desperation. But it would have been madness to doubt her at that moment, when he was returning with a heart so wearied by desire for sympathy. Ralph Cornet refused to do so. Already he was with her in spirit--a tender smile sat on her lips, the first it had worn for months, and once he stretched out his arms to embrace her--he thought she had forgiven him. From the luxury of this dream he was aroused suddenly by a pistol shot, the ball from which whistled not two inches above his head. Before he had time to conjecture whence it came, he was set upon by three men who rushed out from a dark wood, and endeavored to drag him from his horse. Maintaining with difficulty, his position, Ralph laid about him lustily with the end of the gun he still carried. One of the men was soon laid on the ground with the blood spouting from his nostrils, but the other two returned furiously to the attack with drawn swords. Thus pressed upon both sides, he bore up under several wounds, and kept his seat in spite of the curveting of his frightened horse; but at length he was run nearly through the body, and was obliged to clasp his arms around the horse's neck to prevent falling. The assailants now made sure of him, and seized the horse to stop his plunging, but Ralph, with all his remaining strength, struck the spurs into his sides, and the enraged animal broke away with a terrific snort dashing those who held him to the ground, and the next minute the waters hissed and foamed where he plunged in and beat them like something mad or wild with terror.

Ralph held on mechanically during the passage of the river, but when the horse bounded to the bank and shook the water from his flanks, his stiffened limbs were loosed, and he fell motionless to the ground. The men on the other side, who, having been advised of his return by one who had rode on before him, had waylaid him there with determined revenge, now seeing him fall dead as they supposed, took no further interest in the matter, and Ralph Cornet would have died there as he lay if Providence had not so ordained that the African slave, who had moved his dwelling higher up the river since his master's death, should discover him as he was out that evening gathering wood to warm his lonely cabin.

Poor old Juba let his fagots fall, and lifted up his hands and eyes in amazement at the sight of that bloody and inanimate form. At first he sat down and wept over him, but perceiving that the heart still beat, he made an effort to bear him off. The old negro stopped almost in despair at finding how incompetent he was to the task; but he could not give up his beloved young master to die there in the sharp, wintry night air, and after a long time, by lifting and dragging, he brought him to his dwelling. There he laid him on a pallet of fresh straw, and warmed him and dressed his wound with a care, which, if it was not surgeonly, was at least tender and kind.

Ralph awoke in a delirious fever, which raged many days. His faithful servant was terrified at his incoherent words and the violence of his gestures; but he was discreet enough not to hazard his chance of recovery by applying to his enemies for relief. He took the horse into the island, where he fed him secretly, and then went on his way as usual to escape suspicion. He applied the herbs and roots of which the simple pharmacy of his country is composed, to the wounds of Ralph, and trusted to his strong natural system for the rest. It was triumphant at last, and after some time he looked around and knew where he was; but when he attempted to rise he fell back powerless. Many weeks he lay there in the slow, lingering torture of recovery. He heard the birds singing without, and felt the fresh breeze of spring, but could not drag his weakened limbs to the door.

His suspense with regard to Annette rather retarded his convalescence. He had learnt that she was in the fort not far off, and he pined at the thought of being so near without being able to see or hear from her. His days and nights were taken up in contriving some method of informing her of his existence, with which, however, he could trust no one but himself; and his first impulse, soon as he was able to crawl out, was to watch around the fort. On the night that General Pickens saw him there, in that sad and feeble condition, he had ventured to throw a lock of Annette's hair, which he had preserved through all his trials, over the wall, feeling assured that if she saw it she would not fail to recognize it. But after that interview, he deemed it necessary to change his dwelling, for he supposed that a search would be instituted for him, and he was no longer able to resist if discovered.

He built a camp far in the woods, where Andrew Morrison, who had been in search of him for a week, came upon him on the morning of the burial. Ralph's heart melted down at the relation of the forlorn and affecting situation of Annette, and as he heard the kind and soothing words of the old Scotchman, he began to feel the reviving influence of hope. "I will see her at all risks!" he said. Accordingly he stationed himself where he could watch the course of the burial, naturally supposing that she would be the last at the grave; and her stay offered him the opportunity, which he was determined at all hazards to seize.

CHAPTER IX

"There's a divinity that shapes our ends
Rough hew them how we may."

SUCH was the tale of his varied fortunes, which Ralph Cornet recounted to the gentle and pitying girl. She could not but feel how different he was from the light-hearted being who had first fascinated her young fancy. How changed in heart and manners even from the proud and brilliant officer, who six months before sat almost on that very spot at her feet, so handsome, so buoyant with hopes; but never, never in the sunny days of their unclouded love, had he felt so endeared to her as now. Like the gentle Desdemona, she "loved him for the dangers he had passed," and though she saw him thwarted in his prospects, sad and subdued in spirit, friendless and homeless, she would not have left him for the proudest prince on earth; for the deeper the desolation the more does woman cling to the forsaken.

When Annette returned to the fort, she buried herself in the seclusion of her tent, and asked advice of no one on the important step she was about to take. She did not repent of having promised to fly with him, but the future presented to her view a dark uncertainty, which even love, in her present mournful state, could not cheer, and she awaited her destiny in a kind of gloomy apathy. If it is true that "coming events cast their shadows before," it was a forerunner of the dreadful despair she was doomed soon to experience.

Selina Anderson was near her, with all the comfort that a tender heart can suggest for such deep affliction, but Annette turned from her and wept. She could not resolve to discover to that proud and noble girl that she was about to marry the disgraced and exiled man. Mrs. Cornet, who was necessarily in the secret, strengthened Annette in the resolution. It would be hard to say what were the feelings of this lady towards her unfortunate brother-in-law. She had always loved him, and notwithstanding her elevated spirit scorned the part he had acted, she was pleased to hear that he meditated an escape from the dangers which surrounded him. She felt a tender friendship for Annette, but nature spoke still stronger in her heart for him, and she was soothed to think that his exile would not be solitary.

Before night Andrew Morrison was observed to leave the fort with the French Minister, and return alone into the tent of Annette Bruyésant. This, though, was no unusual circumstance and excited no suspicion.

Everything seemed to be propitious for their escape. The gate was closed, and the garrison had retired early to rest. It was a dark night, excepting the faint light of the stars, for "the moon's sweet crescent" was only seen glimmering through the thick trees on the water's edge.

Ralph had appointed to come early, and already a rope was thrown over the wall, which Andrew Morrison fixed to the ground by a stake, and then cautiously helped the trembling girl to ascend. From the top of the wall they observed two men standing in the dark shadow below, and scarcely had Annette set her foot on the ground, when one of them rushed forward and seized her.

Not a word had been spoken on either side, but Annette gave a faint scream, and old Andrew noticed as they moved off with her, that neither of them had the stature of Ralph Cornet. The old Scotchman stood transfixed with horror, and his first thought was to alarm the garrison; for what could he do, an old man, with those desperate ruffians?

But the avenger was at hand! Ralph Cornet was also approaching, when he heard the scream, and in an instant he was on the spot. One brief word of alarm and he was flying off in the direction of the river; but at that moment two men, who had been placed there for the purpose, advanced from the wall and seized him. Ralph felt for his sword, and discovered that he was perfectly unarmed. In the rapturous excitement under which he had set off, he had forgotten even the dagger he thought it prudent to wear usually. But he shook off the grasp of those men as Samson did the Philistines, who seeing him thus escape, discharged their muskets after him by an appointed signal. At the same time on the banks of the river stood the man who yet grasped Annette with his left arm, and the poor girl's head leaned against his shoulder, for she had fainted. The light of the moon's silver horn fell clear upon the features of Hugh Bates. They were fearfully agitated.

"Quick, quick, Miller, and be damned to you!" said he. "Don't you hear those guns? He is coming!"

There was some difficulty in unfastening a canoe. One moment more and Hugh Bates had forever bid him defiance; but Ralph Cornet was now standing face to face with his deadliest enemy. His fierce grasp was on the shoulder of Bates, and with the other hand he seized the insensible form of Annette.

"Villain!" he exclaimed, in a voice hoarse with rage, "yield her to me!"

The eyes of Bates blazed like a wolf's in the dark.

"In death, then!" he muttered, gnashing his teeth, and a dagger gleamed in the moonlight over the breast of Annette. But Ralph Cornet saw the flashing of the blade, and letting go his hold of Annette, he seized the uplifted arm, and with his other hand grasped the throat of the murderer. Bates writhed under the pain, and in an effort of desperation he turned his pliant limbs around the form of Ralph and drew him to the ground. Long and desperate then became the struggle for the dagger. Bates, strong and active at any time, was in the healthy vigor of manhood, almost too much for the enfeebled strength of Cornet. Once in the contest the dagger dropped on the ground, and the quick hands of Bates had seized it, and aimed with deadly precision at the throat of his adversary. But Ralph grasped his wrist with both hands, and directed it to his heart! The limbs of Bates slowly relaxed their clasping hold, and he lay there a stiffening corpse.

When Ralph Cornet rose from that awful conflict, his first thought was of Annette, but she was gone; and possessed of a madness such as he had never before experienced, he rushed to the fort. Already he was mounting the ladder which had been left there, but the still vigorous arm of Andrew Morrison was laid upon him.

"Haud, haud, man! wad ye rin to yer destruction?" said he.

"Begone!" exclaimed Ralph, impatiently dashing the old man aside.

But he still laid hold of him.

"Are ye mad?" he asked. "Ralph Cornet, do you wish to die in ane moment mair? If not for my sake, for the sake o' her wha loes ye, forbear. She is nae there, it may be."

It was the first time that Ralph had thought of that. He sunk back to the ground, and a fierce convulsive shaking seized him. He looked as if he were finding refuge in death. Andrew Morrison wiped the cold perspiration from his brow, and as he unbuttoned his collar to give him air, he perceived a stream of blood upon his bosom.

"Mercy!" exclaimed he, in surprise. "Ye hae been wounded then, my puir bairn?"

"It is the blood of Bates!" said Ralph, shivering as he related the distressing event which had occurred.

Every hour of his life seemed to bring curses on the head of the unfortunate man. But the bitterest drop in that bitter cup was the mysterious disappearance of Annette, and his own disability to seek for her and revenge the outrage done to her.

The old man, seeing the pitiful situation into which he had fallen, attempted consolation, and endeavored to inspire a hope which he hardly felt himself.

"Tak' heart, tak' heart, my boy!" said he. "Ye shall hae her yet! On the word o' an auld man, ye shall hae her yet! That Bates was an awfu' man, an' yer mortal enimy. Ye hae done weel in ridding the airth o' a villainy. Besides, ye could nae help what ye hae done, when the black wretch was drawing, as ain may say, the verri life's bluid o' yer heart. But be thankfu', my lad; he canna disturb ye mair, an' ye shall hae her yet."

But Ralph could not wipe away from his memory that stain of blood. He was shocked at the dire necessity which imposed it on him, and maddened that it involved the destruction of his plans. He dared still less than ever to appear before his countrymen, for few of them knew as well as he the black villainy of Hugh Bates, and still fewer, he was assured, would look with unprejudiced eyes on the circumstances attending his death.

Ralph Cornet knew not himself the whole extent to which that villainy aimed in its accomplishment; he, as well as Annette, was ignorant of the agency which Bates had had in her father's death, and his appearance at this time and interference in a plan which Ralph believed he had projected in secret, was a mystery which he could not unravel. Had Ralph been quick enough in that last interview by the cottage, to have heeded the words of the child, that mystery might have been explained, or rather anticipated. There was an eye upon those lovers--not less envious, not less malicious, than that with which the serpent regarded the first two that ever found a paradise on earth, and that was the eye of Hugh Bates.

After that unsuccessful pursuit of Ralph Cornet, when he had given him up as lost, Bates maintained the character of a good whig by following the American army. In this he had literally no choice, since to be shot as a deserter on one side, or as a traitor on the other, was equally impending if he had been captured. But when, after the battle of Cowpens, he returned into the neighborhood, he was left by his own request with the guard of the fort. There, from often seeing Annette, his former passion had revived, and he dared once more to look upon her with an eye of love. But seeing that the gentle girl treated him with a scorn she never exhibited to others, he only waited an opportunity to revenge on her this contempt for his passion. The death of her father he imagined would place her more securely in his power, and he was laying a train for her in his mind on returning from Vienna, after having calmly attended the burial of him he had sent to the grave, when he heard voices back of the cottage, and crept up closely to reconnoitre. There he saw the man whom he believed dead, with his arms around his intended victim, and heard her vow to be another's. If he had been armed with a rifle, that would have been the last moment of Ralph Cornet, but he had no arms except the dagger which he always wore; and though fierce as a tiger when roused, he dreaded nothing more than a personal encounter with Ralph. He held his breath gaspingly as the plot of Annette's escape was revealed to him, and clenching his fist firmly, he muttered between his grinding teeth--

"To-morrow night!--then to-morrow night I shall be avenged!"

He returned to the fort, and permitted things to pass off in their usual course; for Hugh Bates knew well the art of dissembling.

But in the meantime he was busily maturing his plan, which was to anticipate Ralph in carrying off Annette.

"I, too, can fly with her," said he. "When we are off she shall be mine in spite of her, and I shall be gloriously avenged on both."

With these views he informed the garrison that at a particular place they might take Ralph Cornet, whom they had believed dead, and having excused himself from the party on the plea of private business, he left the fort a little before dark, with one man, to whom he entrusted his scheme. He felt very certain that the enmity of the men was sufficient to ensure the death of Cornet, but he advised them if there was any danger of his escape to fire for assistance.

As to his own private matter--determined that his revenge should be felt even in spite of death--he directed Miller, the man who accompanied him, in case anything happened to himself, to fly with Annette to some place of concealment.

The next morning the body of Bates was found and buried on the spot. His fate excited but little sympathy with those who believed in his guilt, as the story was told by Andrew Morrison; but a vigorous search was instituted for Ralph Cornet, and the place of Annette's imprisonment kept closely veiled.

On the same day of Bates' burial intelligence arrived at the fort of the death of the gallant Lieut. Pickens. He was picked off by a rifleman before the siege of Ninety-Six. As he had expressed it, he died "beloved and regretted," but he did not live to see the victory for which he had so nobly contended. The mournful pressure of events which immediately followed his death almost erased the memory of his loss; for the lonely spot where his grave was dug soon became a burying ground for soldiers like himself. But there was one heart which raised a proud monument to his name. As the freshness of grief wore away in the bosom of Selina Anderson, the pride of his memory rose in her soul. Yes, she could bear to talk with a tearless eye of him who slept.

> *"As sleeps the brave who sink to rest,*
> *By all their country's wishes blest."*

CHAPTER X

"Why, let the stricken deer go weep,
The hart ungalled play;
For some must watch, whilst some must sleep--
So runs the world away."
SHAKSPEARE.

"She's won! we are off, over bank, bush and scaur, They'll have fleet
steeds that follow,' quoth young Lochinvar."

IT was a day of public rejoicing at Vienna. Some part of the scattered remnant of the American soldiery had returned from Eutaw into that neighborhood. The victory was nearly decided, and the voice of exultation, which rose over the wail of widows and orphans and drowned the groans of the dying, told to every surrounding echo that the country was free!

What a day was that for the small remnant of whig militia--that firm patriotic band, which had withstood temptations and distress, poverty and hardships of every degree--men who left their families in the hands of a murderous banditti at home and went forth to meet the foe–

"Firm as a rock of the ocean that stems a thousand wild waves by the shore"-- and who having now returned to witness the woeful devastation created in their absence, could only clasp their few remaining treasures and say, "These are mine own!" It was both a proud and a bitter day for them; but they were conquerors. The foe was retreating from the country, and with the natural sympathies of men who have been associated, and come safely out of some dangerous enterprise, they met with hearts and tongues overflowing with the dangers they had passed.

The day was in sultry June, and the burning sun which had seemed to set on fire the low painted roofs of the houses of Vienna, shed an oblique radiance upon the western windows, which were now opened to admit the cool breeze springing up from the river. The single street as well as the houses was thronged with men--under the shade of trees--in the piazzas--sitting, standing, walking, laughing and shouting--in every variety of rude and careless happiness. Some stood about in groups resting on their guns, which from long habit had become necessary to their comfort; whilst some one of the number, swelling with the importance of fancied advantage over the rest, told with a boastful air the tale of his "deeds in arms," how he had fought in such a battle, or how he had gulled such a tory. All of which his auditors approved by loud laughing and significant gestures. But it was observed that none laughed so loud as those who had the most doubtful right to sympathise with the speaker; for though the pride of the whigs, together with the recent wrongs they had suffered at their hands, caused them to scorn all offers of friendship from the crest fallen tories, there were yet very many among that class, who, by a prudent caution, had reserved themselves a place among the conquering party. Many of these now mingled with the under class of whigs who filled the grog shops with bacchanalian revelry, and it was not uncommon to see a boasting whig who had advanced into the highest state of quarrelsome intermeddling, step out, and rolling up the sleeves from his brawny arms, challenge another man to prove himself not a tory. It was all a scene of noise and bustle--a true picture of the disorders and license of a state of recent warfare, and a natural evidence of the haughtiness with which man assumed power. Some others of the younger men even, who had rested their guns against the houses, and engaged in the peaceful game of running, wrestling or ball-playing, whenever a man was seen passing along the road at a distance, or skulking under the bushes, would shout the word "Tory!" from one to the other, and chase him out of sight, with the loud laugh and broad halloo of childish delight. As the fox which has been the terror of the farm-yard, after having been run down and disarmed of its power by the huntsman, is crowed and cackled over by the delighted fowls, and pelted with stones and pulled about by the revengeful children, thus these deluded beings, no longer feared, were become the butt of the conquering party--objects merely deserving the indignities of contempt. There was only one, who by the high character of his bold and lofty defiance, seemed to be worthy of their resentment. He had baffled and evaded them. His indomitable spirit refused to sue or submit, and though he had committed fewer deeds of abhorrence than any one of the vile class with whom he had been associated, his countrymen hated him with the deepest and most deadly hatred; for the tyrannical heart of man is too haughty in the hour of victory to suffer any defiance. But Ralph Cornet, by the superior finesse of his motions, had as yet eluded their grasp. They hunted him as the wild beast is hunted in the wilds of Africa, with sword and spear, but though he was known to be yet in the neighborhood, no hand could be laid upon him.

Thus thwarted, his enemies had but one way of revenging themselves. It is true they had seized his broad lands on the Savannah by sequestration, but they knew that the only way to wring the soul of Ralph was to deprive him of his betrothed--his beloved Annette. And, however strange it may appear, it is no less true that this arbitrary measure against an innocent and unoffending girl, was put into rigid execution.

As the evening advanced, however, a party of the conquerors, a part from these, were preparing for a more refined species of enjoyment. A large room of a house on the bank of the river, was filled to crowding with people of both sexes. It was the same room in which the brave Pickens sat a few months before when he gave audience to the wily Bates. They were both gone; the noble patriot and the vile intriguer had alike sunk into the vortex of the stream which deluged their country, and there upon the very spot where they had concerted plans of such vital interest to one of them at least, their survivors, with that strange insensibility to death which always attends times of danger, were making merry. A ring was cleared in the centre of the room for dancing, and as the fiddler entered and began the tantalizing exercise of calling into order his rebellious strings, giving every now and then an encouraging twitch of the elbow over the shrieking catgut, the young men jumped up in eager anticipation and capered about the room. Some were in white stockings and pumps, with yellow small clothes, which they had just purchased from some itinerant merchant peddling through the country; but most of them wore their high-heeled boots, with yellow tops turned over from the tights of Kersey or homespun, which had perhaps borne the brunt of war. Nevertheless, each one felt himself irresistible in the eyes of the young ladies, who, silly creatures, simpered and whispered among each other, still casting timid and lively glances at their invincible warriors.

But there was one countenance in that assembly which moved not for all that merriment, no more than if it had fallen on the dull, cold ear of death. It was the pale face of Annette Bruyésant, who sat in one corner, far as possible from the revellers, in the stiff and rigid attitude of marble. No motion betrayed the vitality which animated that statue. No tear, no sigh, no glance evinced the sensibilities of a wounded spirit. But her eyes were fixed upon the opposite window in the cold glassy gaze of despair, and her hands were folded in her lap in the mute eloquence of submission.

As the dancing went on she was left alone. No one was sufficiently hard-hearted to insult her misery by asking her to join them. She had only been forced to attend her guardians there, for fear some effort should be made for her escape in their absence.

The time was past when that sweet girl could make any resistance, and she was now perfectly passive in the hands of her persecutors. If she felt, she showed no resentment towards them. She might perhaps have approved the justness of Ralph Cornet's condemnation--she never for a moment thought of forsaking him. No, the more wretched an outcast he became, the more did that faithful girl believe it her duty to cling to him; and as she sat in that apparently apathetic posture, her thoughts were bound up in a painful dream. But it was not of herself she was thinking. It was of him--of his griefs, and loneliness, and dangers. Could she have thrown herself in his arms at that moment, the language of her heart would have been:

"Thou hast called me thine angel in moments of bliss,
Still thine angel I'll be 'mid the horrors of this."

But despair, despair of ever seeing him was doing its dreadful work there, and her heart continued to weep its drops of blood. In this situation she did not perceive that any one approached her until she felt herself touched lightly on the shoulder, and, turning round, she met the eyes of Andrew Morrison for the first time since her captivity, who, with a cautious look around them, dropped a piece of paper in her hand. Annette grasped the paper and turned her back instinctively on the company. A fearful change came over her face as she devoured the scrawl. It merely contained the words in rude characters--

"Be at the window an hour hence. I shall be there."

The blood rushed into Annette's face until it became lurid, and her veins swelled until they were visible on the surface of her beautiful forehead. Then again she became ghastly pale, and gasped for breath. As she turned to speak to the old man the words died away with a choking noise in her throat. But Andrew Morrison had left her side. The wary old man knew that suspicion already rested upon him, and upon his caution now depended the success of his undertaking. At this time a very different scene was acting in a house exactly opposite that in which the ball was going on. There a wounded man lay upon a pallet on the floor to get the cool air of evening, and his head rested on the bosom of a handsome woman, who was pulling back the thick masses of raven hair from his brow. As she did so, the tears fell from her heavy eyelids on the worn and wasted features of the dying man.

"My own Ellen!" said he, as he wiped off the tears from his face, "do not weep so, you will kill me before my time by your grief."

"Oh, James!" said she, in a voice which was racked with anguish, "how can I help it, to hear all this noise and rejoicing, and you lying here?"

"Do not let that disturb you, my love," replied her husband, with a faint attempt at smiling. "It is the nature of man to forget in prosperity the means by which he gained it. Why should I think to be remembered more than the thousands who lie on the field of battle?"

"Oh, but James, they might respect you while that you are living--you who are dying for them, as I may say." And she burst into a fresh agony of tears.

"No, Ellen, no," answered the dying man with fervor. "I die for the cause--the glorious cause! And--," he continued, his faded eyes sparkling with some of their wonted brilliancy, "and we are free! thank heaven, we are free!"

As the glow of enthusiasm died away from the hollow cheek of the soldier, he sunk back exhausted, and lay for some time silent. It was evident his hour was fast approaching. His breath at times came thick and gaspingly, and his eyes rolled upward. But the sobs of his wife seemed again to disturb him.

"Ellen!" said he, almost in a whisper "my good Ellen--you have always been kind to me! Do not grieve so if you would have me die contented. I could have wished--but no matter. It is God's will, and I have but one wish on earth--it is to see my poor Ralph before I die. It is too late now. But you said that Annette Bruyésant was here. Send for her that I may tell her--tell her I forgive him."

A few minutes after Annette had read the paper and resumed her seat with apparent calmness, a little boy made his way through the crowd and threw himself on her lap, crying bitterly. All that could be extracted from him was that his father was dying and wished to see Annette Bruyésant. It was a sight to have melted a heart of stone, and these hearts already softened by the sweetness of Annette's temper, could not refuse her this sad duty.

She followed the child across the street, almost surprised at the liberty granted her.

So soon as she was gone Andrew Morrison also left the room, but there was no heed given to his actions--the amusements went on unabated.

By the time Annette reached the house some of his former friends were gathered round the pallet of the dying soldier; but he paid them no attention. His gaze was fixed on Annette as she knelt beside him, her eyes, before so cold and motionless, now streaming with tears. He clasped her hand with all his remaining strength and his lips moved, but Annette heard no sound until she leaned her ear close to his face.

"You will see him," said he, in broken sentences; "tell him--my brother--that--I loved him to the last!"

He now struggled for utterance--a low gurgling sound was heard in his throat, and his wife threw herself in distraction on his breast. But he opened his eyes--

"Ellen--my boy--where is Willie?" The child crept up, and

put his little hand into that of his father. "Make him a soldier--you hear that, Ellen-- and--raise me a little higher, love--it is dark here--and--do not--let him be--a--a traitor--to--to--." His voice failed him, and his head sunk on his breast.

In a few minutes the soldier's children were orphans; for James Cornet lay there a corpse, one of the noblest victims to the battle of Eutaw.

Annette threw her arms around the widowed mother--the kind soother of her own bereavement--and wept long with her. At length she arose and walked out upon the piazza. The street was still busy with its crowd, and the sound of that music with the heavy tramp of the dancers came to her ear. Her heart sickened, and she leaned against a column for support. Then the thought of her own uncertain destiny came over her mind with agonizing force, and she envied the man who, in that chamber of death, was released so easily and happily from a world which appeared so dark to her.

At that moment a horseman was seen ascending the hill of that thronged street, in full view of the windows of the ball-room. He was riding a horse of prodigious size and beauty, which seemed to yield to every motion of the rider, as his graceful swanlike neck obeyed the impulse of the rein.

Annette raised her clasped hands to heaven, and stood with her lips apart, all her blood curdling with surprise and terror. She remembered the paper she had received. It was the appointed hour, and it could be no other than Ralph Cornet. But would even he dare thus much?

The men who filled the streets stood regarding the approaching stranger with surprise greater than her's. The hand of every man dropped on his gun, but remained there motionless, and a death-like silence reigned where all before was confusion--so great was the curiosity and awe which that majestic horseman excited as he galloped fearlessly as it were against the very bayonets of his enemies. The keen eye of Ralph had descried that well known form, and in an instant he stood by the door, all unconscious how nearly he was connected with the painful scene within. "Haste, haste, Annette!" said he, and he pulled the fainting form of the poor girl to his saddlebow. One touch of the rein, and the proud animal, as if conscious of his master's triumph, arched his high neck, and with a bound flew towards the river bank. Then, as if some spell of enchantment had been loosed, the men moved from every part of the village. Every gun was raised, and curses rang on the name of Ralph Cornet. But by the time they reached the river's side the noble horse was beating the waters with his broad breast, far into the middle of the current.

Why did not these men fire? There was not one but knew from the first that it was Ralph Cornet. Was it a sympathy with the beautiful and simple boldness of this action which deterred them? Or, was it the native horror which man has against interfering with anything already in the hands of God? Certain it is that they saw those two beings, who had suffered so long, piteously struggling there in the midst of that wide river, and not a gun was discharged. But when that noble animal bounded, drippingly, on the opposite shore, with his brave and beautiful burden, a low and suppressed murmur of admiration and astonishment ran along that crowd of men, which only a few moments before were breathing curses.

For a moment did Ralph Cornet pause and turn his gaze upon the spot he had left behind. Annette lay with her arms around him, and he bent over and kissed her cheek as it were in defiance. A wild, a joyous, a triumphant laugh rang over the waters as the horse wheeled round and was seen bounding along, for some distance, under the dark shadowy trees, extending out from the high grassy bank. Ralph Cornet had turned his back forever on his country. In a sweet sequestered spot, where a little stream wound along through grassy banks, and where a rustic bridge was half overhung with a canopy of pendant vines, Andrew Morrison, that faithful friend, was awaiting them with the French minister. The sun was just sinking below the trees, and the sweet birds, lifting up their voices in the chorus of evening, sang the marriage hymn of Ralph Cornet and his Annette. After so much suffering and trial, he felt himself amply compensated when he clasped her to his bosom--his own!

They then bid those last and dear friends adieu, and were turning to depart, when a strange and somewhat ludicrous figure started up from against a tree, exclaiming, in an humble but reproachful accent:

"Massa Ralph, no lebe ole nigger stay here, eh?"

"No, my good Juba, no," said Ralph. "You shall go if you wish it."

"Ha, ha!" laughed the African. "Ole nigger go for true. No stay here for dam tory gun--whiplash. Juba follow his massa to eend ob de world." And slinging his huge bundle on a stick across his shoulder, old Juba trudged on after the only being he loved on earth.

The world of Ralph Cornet's acquaintance was lost in conjecture. Even his enemies would have given up their resentment for some knowledge of that bold and extraordinary man. But the old Scotchman was the only depository of that secret, and to his dying day he never revealed the place where the British Partizan carried his bride.